TOUKAN
THE FIRST FALLING

M.J. SAEED

PASSIONPRENEUR® PUBLISHING

Publishing information

Publishing and design facilitated by Passionpreneur Publishing
A division of Passionpreneur Organization Pty Ltd
ABN: 48640637529
Melbourne, VIC | Australia
www.passionpreneurpublishing.com

To the readers, this world now belongs to you

THE
FIRST FALLING

M.J. SAEED

TABLE OF CONTENTS

CHAPTER ONE
The First Falling

The land of Alard was no ordinary realm. It breathed mystery, held secrets beneath its soil, and pulsed with an ancient energy woven into the very essence of life itself. For generations, it stood as a land of deep power and deeper silence—its beauty hiding the weight of something vast and unseen.

What made Alard unlike any other land was the force flowing through every living human. Its people—every single one of them—were born with something extraordinary deep within their flesh.

Reiki.

Every human born in Alard carried Reiki within them, etched into their bodies from the moment they took their first breath. It wasn't magic. It wasn't a blessing from the heavens. It was life itself.

Through harsh, relentless training, a person could strengthen their Reiki and use it to gain incredible physical abilities—inhuman speed, strength, and endurance far beyond the reach of an ordinary person.

Yet there existed a deeper level of power—an unreachable summit for most.

Awakening.

To awaken your Reiki was something else entirely. It was not something achieved through discipline alone. It required a kind of breaking—a refinement of body and spirit that only a handful in all of Alard's history had ever endured. An awakened Reiki did not just enhance someone's power—it changed them. Transformed them. Elevated them.

Most people, no matter how hard they trained, would never awaken their Reiki. The gap between a skilled Reiki fighter and one who had an awakened Reiki was like the distance between land and sky.

In the early days, Alard was unified; there was no order. Those with stronger Reiki often used their power to commit crimes—murder, theft, and acts of senseless destruction. With no ruler, no law to answer to, chaos spread across the land like wildfire. Villages burned. Families disappeared. Fear ruled.

And so the Royal clans stepped forward.

But these clans were not Royal by crown, bloodline, or wealth. Their status came from something greater: their Reiki. Their Reiki was different—more potent and tied directly to the forces of nature.

Each clan possessed its own elemental affinity:

- *The Toukan Clan mastered wind.* 

- *The Akaryu Clan wielded fire.* 

- *The Laitonn Clan commanded lightning.* 

- *The Abahare Clan moved with water.* 

The leaders of the four clans gathered for the first time in generations. It was not a council of ceremony—it was a council of survival.

Tension filled the air.

Each clan brought its own concerns, its own philosophies. The Akaryu demanded swift justice. The Laitonn sought strength through force. The Abahare called for patience and measured strategy. And the Toukan, led by Ujitaka Toukan, spoke little—but when he did, the others listened.

Ujitaka Toukan was not the loudest among them. He did not carry himself like a man desperate for leadership. He was calm, collected, and measured in every word and movement. But his presence was undeniable. His awakened Reiki, and command over wind, was unmatched.

More than that, his leadership had already brought peace to the region under Toukan protection.

UJITAKA TOUKAN

He had earned respect through action, not ambition.

After days of deliberation, it became clear: If anyone could restore balance to Alard, it was Ujitaka.

And so the decision was made.

He was named the ruler of Alard—not as a king with a crown, but as a protector, a guardian whose purpose was to uphold order, peace, and justice. A man not above the clans, but chosen to hold them together.

Ujitaka brought peace.

Under his leadership, Alard became civilized. He united the clans. He enforced Law. He protected the weak. The land that once bled now began to breathe. For the first time in years, people began to live without fear.

But not all were pleased.

A lesser clan—the Seher Clan—despised what Alard had become. They rejected peace. They hated the idea of one man ruling the land. While the Royal clans refined their elemental Reiki, the Seher Clan specialized in Dark Reiki—a corrupted form of energy born from hatred, pain, and envy.

They believed they were owed more than the world had ever given them. And they intended to take it.

In secret, the clan gathered every ounce of their remaining Dark Reiki and began preparing a ritual—an ancient one. A ritual spoken only in the oldest scrolls, long dismissed as myth. It was a ritual of self-sacrifice that destroyed their own bodies and summoned something far worse in return.

When the final words of the summoning were spoken, the air itself trembled. A wave of dark energy surged through the land. Trees bent to the ground. The skies grew silent. The earth cracked. Even the animals fled.

And then—it came.

A Being not born of Alard, nor shaped by its laws. Something far older. Far worse.

The Mutotsu.

THE MUTOTSU

It didn't arrive with flames or thunder. It stepped into the world like it had always belonged—like it had simply been waiting to return.

What followed was destruction.

The Mutotsu moved with purpose, destroying anything that stood in its path. Villages were wiped from the map. Entire families were killed before they even understood what they faced. Nothing could stand before it.

No weapons could pierce it. No barrier could slow it down. The strongest warriors fell; all attacks were useless. Even the Royal clans struggled to comprehend what they were seeing.

It was clear: This was not a threat they would overcome.

But before all hope was lost, one man stepped forward.

When the world seemed on the brink of collapse, one man stood between Alard and total ruin.

Ujitaka Toukan.

He didn't wait for a war council. He didn't gather an army. He simply stepped forward.

Ujitaka was the only member of the Toukan Clan who had awakened his Reiki at the time. Ujitaka faced the Mutotsu head-on. The clash between them shook the land. Storms gathered. Winds howled. Every strike from Ujitaka tore through the air like a blade, but the Mutotsu was unlike any enemy he—or anyone—had ever faced.

It couldn't be killed.

No matter how precise his techniques or how overwhelming his Reiki, nothing could destroy it. Blow after blow landed with full force, but the creature endured, pressing forward without slowing.

And then he understood.

The Mutotsu couldn't be destroyed. Not by strength. Not by force. It was a being that existed beyond the natural order—something that didn't belong in the world. He knew it couldn't be killed.

But it could be sealed.

Drawing on the most sacred and forbidden technique of the Toukan Clan, Ujitaka prepared a sealing method—a powerful ability that only those in the Toukan Clan with awakened Reiki could possess.

It was not a simple technique, as it required far more than energy—in fact, it demanded the life of the one who cast it.

To trap something like the Mutotsu, the user had to offer themselves up as the foundation of the seal. Their soul, their awakened Reiki—all bound into the technique to keep it intact.

Ujitaka knew this.

And he didn't hesitate.

With his final breath, he called forth the winds of his ancestors. The earth cracked beneath him. A vortex of spiritual force erupted into the sky, wrapping around the Mutotsu and pulling it into a prison of pure energy.

The Mutotsu vanished.

The winds calmed.

And when the dust settled...Ujitaka was dead.

The people of Alard mourned the man who had saved Alard. His name became legend, his sacrifice carved into the memory of every generation that followed.

Though the sealing of the Mutotsu had spared Alard from complete destruction, the danger it posed did not vanish with its body. Even as Ujitaka's life was consumed by the sacred technique that bound the creature, the Mutotsu ensured that its own end would not be final.

At the moment the seal took hold, the Mutotsu released a final surge of energy— not in panic, but with clear intent. From its body erupted four glass plates, each one pulsing faintly with a shard of its dark essence. The plates scattered across the land, spreading throughout Alard.

The four plates were far more than fragments of a vanquished power—they were part of a carefully planted safeguard. Though the seal had held, it was never meant to last forever. There were two paths by which the Mutotsu could return. One was through time itself. As the years passed, the seal would slowly weaken, and after 100 years it would begin to loosen, allowing the creature to reemerge on its own. The other path was more immediate—and far more dangerous. If all the four plates were recovered and brought back together, the seal could be broken by force, unleashing the Mutotsu long before its natural release, and bring it back at full strength.

But the Mutotsu's preparation didn't end with the plates.

Far from the battlefield, in quite an unassuming region of Alard, lived a man named Shen Danbu. He had no place among the warriors, no link to the Royal clans, and no awareness of the catastrophe that had just been narrowly averted—yet it was he whom the Mutotsu marked.

Its dark energy, guided by intent, travelled across the land and found Shen, not by accident, but by choice. It did not tear through him with destruction, nor did it manifest with violence. It entered him quietly, slipping into the core of his being like a shadow settling into place. It was not a curse. It was a transfer—an inheritance.

And from that moment on, Shen Danbu was no longer fully human.

SHEN DANBU

He became the first Mutant.

The first Mutahawl.

There was no madness in him, no change in thought or identity. Shen remained fully aware—his mind intact, his memories unclouded—but something deep within had undeniably changed. It wasn't loud or violent; it was quiet and absolute. A different motive had settled within his core, so seamlessly woven into his consciousness that he could no longer distinguish it from his own.

With that purpose came strength—unnatural and immense. The Dark Reiki given to him by the Mutotsu surged through his body like a second life force, transforming his essence and vastly increasing his power. He had become something far more dangerous than he ever imagined.

Now, he moved towards a single goal:

Revive the Mutotsu.

He would not walk that path alone.

That dark energy that now lived within him carried more than strength—it also carried contagion. Shen possessed the ability to extend his transformation to others. With a touch of his Dark Reiki, he could infect human souls, bending their memories, their thoughts, and the faces they once wore, until their allegiance was no longer their own. It had been quietly replaced by the will of something far older, far more commanding.

Together, the Mutahawls moved with a shared purpose:

To reclaim the four glass plates scattered across Alard, then bring them back in place to break the seal and awaken the Mutotsu before its time.

In order to grow stronger, they hunted—not to feed, but to take.

Mutahawls did not consume human flesh or feast on their victims like beasts. They killed with intent. Each death allowed them to absorb the slain person's Reiki, converting it into dark Reiki that deepened their power and drew them closer to their goal. But death wasn't their only weapon. A Mutahawl could also force its Dark Reiki into a living human, turning them into one of their own. With each person corrupted, their numbers grew—and so did the darkness that followed them.

As the years passed, the number of Mutants—now known across the land as Mutahawls—continued to rise. Slowly and quietly, their presence spread, their numbers multiplying.

It is now the ninetieth year since the sealing of the Mutotsu. Although most of the world moved forward in the belief that peace had been restored, the shadows told a different story.

Alard stands under the rule of a single man: Yuuta Toukan, leader of the Toukan Clan and the most powerful living Reiki warrior of his time. Revered for both his strength and his wisdom, Yuuta earned his place not only through bloodline but through the immense Reiki he wielded—Reiki that, even from a young age, had set him apart from all others.

Unlike those before him, Yuuta had foreseen the lingering threat of the Mutotsu's return. Driven by that awareness, he sought out and successfully recovered all four of the glass plates, scattered long ago during the creature's final moments. One by one, he located them across the furthest corners of Alard, placing each under heavy protection to prevent them from ever falling into the hands of Mutants who might try to revive what must remain buried.

YUUTA TOUKAN

Yuuta was more than a guardian—he was a father. He had three sons, each born with the blood of the Toukan Clan flowing through their veins. The eldest, Ryoze Toukan. The middle son, Tadanaka. The youngest, Yasaze.

Under Yuuta's leadership, the Royal clans stood united. While each possessed its own strength and ancestral domain, they all recognized

Yuuta as the ruler of Alard. To maintain peace and balance across the vast territory, Yuuta divided Alard into four major regions, assigning each to one of the Royal clans as its protector.

The northwest was governed by the Toukan Clan, masters of wind, whose swift and precise Reiki had defended Alard for generations.

The northeast fell under the guardianship of the Abahare Clan, whose mastery over water granted them both defensive resilience and adaptability.

In the southwest, the Laitonn Clan, wielders of lighting, held their ground—known for their explosive speed and unrelenting force.

Lastly, the southeast was entrusted to the Akaryu Clan, born of fire, their strength fierce and burning with an unmatched intensity.

Though each region was under the direct care of its respective clan, all served Yuuta without question. His authority stood above them, not through oppression, but through earned respect. He was not merely the ruler of a nation. He was the one man strong enough to keep the darkness from returning.

But the seal was weakening.

And the century was drawing to a close.

CHAPTER TWO
The Sisters' Vengeance

Hidden deep within the remote stretches of the Toukan region, far from the Reiki warriors' routes and the watchful eyes of the main settlements, stood the remains of an old, forgotten temple. The structure, once a place of quiet reflection, now bore the weight of time—its stone foundations cracked, its walls worn down by wind and rain. Nature had reclaimed much of it, but its silence was broken by the harsh clang of metal striking metal—an echo of the battle unfolding within.

Inside that ruin, two young women trained with relentless fury.

Their movements were swift, calculated, and violent—far more than routine sparring. This was not the practice of students learning form. It was the brutal rhythm of warriors preparing for war. Dust rose from the ground with every impact, echoing the years of rage they had buried within them.

They were sisters.

The older, Kume, carried herself with the poise of someone who had seen too much, her strikes crisp and merciless. Her younger sister, Kuna, though slightly less refined, matched her blow for blow, her speed fueled by something equally intense.

KUME

KUNA

Both had undergone years of harsh training, enduring every hardship they could find in order to develop their Reiki and hone their combat to deadly precision. They were no longer ordinary women—they had forged themselves into weapons.

They did not train for discipline.

They trained for vengeance.

Behind their power, beneath their sharpened instincts, there was a plan. A mission. A pact forged in grief and hate. The two sisters had aligned themselves with a being most humans feared to speak of aloud—a Mutahawl named Gerad.

GERAD

Gerad was no common Mutant. He was the seventh-ranked Member of the Torima—a feared order of elite Mutahawls who had long abandoned what little remained of their humanity. Each Member of the Torima had killed countless humans, absorbed the Reiki of their victims and amplified their own dark power to monstrous levels.

Over time, they had become living vessels of Dark Reiki, walking disasters, unmatched in brutality and strength. And among them, rank was more than number—it was a measure of survival, of power, of kills.

Though Gerad held the seventh rank among the Torima, he was by no means weak. On the contrary, he possessed immense power, having absorbed the Reiki of countless humans and refined it into a formidable force of Dark Reiki. His strength alone made him a threat few could face.

Yet within the Torima, rank was earned through dominance, and those above him held even greater power—stronger, more ruthless, more efficient in their destruction. Gerad understood this hierarchy, but it never diminished his presence. What set him apart was his control—the cold precision, patience, and quiet dread that followed him wherever he went. He was not reckless, nor did he waste his energy on chaos without reason. Gerad moved with purpose, and that made him no less dangerous than those who outranked him.

And Kume and Kuna had chosen to follow him. Not as slaves or puppets, but as allies. Their hatred for the man who ruled Alard was stronger than any fear.

Years ago, Yuuta Toukan—ruler of the land, revered by many as a hero—had ordered the slaughter of their village. The sisters had never forgotten. And they had never forgiven. Whether his actions had been justified no longer mattered. Their world had been shattered, and all that remained was the cold drive to see justice in their own form.

Though still human, Kume and Kuna had thrown away the lives they once knew. Their alliance with Gerad was strategic. If they were to have any chance of confronting the man they hated most, they would need power beyond that of any normal warrior.

Gerad sat beneath the faded arch of the old temple, cloaked in shadow as a cold breeze stirred the dust around him. Opposite him knelt Kume and Kuna, the sisters whose paths had long since diverged from the life they were born into. The flickering light of a dying lantern cast long shadows across the stone floor, giving the gathering an uneasy stillness.

They had been discussing the same subject for days—refining the same plan, reviewing every possibility, every risk. And now, it was time to commit.

"When the moment comes," Gerad said, his voice low and even, "you strike fast, clean, and without hesitation."

Kume nodded, her expression calm but sharp, like a blade left out in the cold for too long. She had always been the stronger of the two sisters—more disciplined, more precise. Where Kuna's emotions sometimes got the better of her, Kume buried hers beneath layers of control, forged through the years of loss and training.

"You'll be the one to move in," Gerad continued, his gaze resting solely on Kume. "We cannot afford recklessness. Yuuta Toukan won't fall easily—not even if he's wounded. This will not be a full assault. It will be a message."

Kume glanced sideways at her younger sister. Kuna's fists were clenched tightly at her sides, her jaw set. She hated being sidelined. But they had discussed this already.

"If anything goes wrong," Gerad added, "you flee. No hesitation. No second attempt. This isn't about dying for revenge—it's about making him bleed, and surviving long enough to do it again."

Kume gave a small nod, eyes steady. She understood the weight of the task. A hit-and-run was all they could manage. To challenge Yuuta directly was suicide. But if she could strike, land a blow, and vanish before retaliation—it would send a message that even he wasn't untouchable.

Kuna looked to her sister, conflicted but silent. She wanted to be the one. She wanted to be there. But in the end, she knew the truth—Kume was faster, more experienced, and more likely to survive.

"I'll do it," Kume said at last, her voice steady. "I'll strike and I'll get out. I won't fail."

Gerad offered a cold smile, barely more than a twitch of his lips.

"Then we wait. The moment will come."

CHAPTER THREE
A Summoning and a Strike

Morning sunlight filtered gently through the Gochuu base, casting golden slivers across the polished wooden floor. The compound, perched high on a quiet ridge within the Toukan region, was unusually still. Its usual rhythm of movement and low conversation was absent—the warriors who filled its halls had been dispatched the day before, and now the air was heavy with silence.

Tadanaka Toukan, the second son of Yuuta, sat alone in the main hall, cross-legged at a low table as steam curled up from a fresh pot of tea. A half-eaten breakfast sat beside him, though his appetite had long since faded. His mind was elsewhere—circling around the brief, unexplained message he had received late the previous night.

His father had summoned him to the castle. No reason given.

Though he wasn't one to jump to conclusions, something about the timing gnawed at him. The Gochuu had only just been deployed.

Tadanaka wasn't just Yuuta's son—he was also the commander of the Gochuu, a powerful team of Reiki warriors personally selected by Yuuta himself. The Gochuu were elite in every respect—highly disciplined, deeply loyal, and known for their precision and strength. They weren't used for ceremonial tasks or grand declarations. They were sent where sharp decisions and stronger hands were required.

And this morning, Tadanaka was the only one left at the base.

The soft slide of a door broke the silence. Footsteps followed—light and familiar. A moment later, Yasaze Toukan entered the room with his usual gentle demeanor, offering a small smile as he joined his older brother at the table.

"You're up early," Tadanaka muttered, without lifting his eyes.

"I smelled tea," Yasaze replied as he took a seat and poured himself a cup.

YASAZE TOUKAN

Unlike his brothers, Yasaze had been born without Reiki—a rare phenomenon unheard of not just in the Toukan line, but in all of Alard. To most, it was considered an anomaly. Some even whispered that it was a flaw. But Yuuta never treated him differently. Yasaze's presence, calm and pure, carried a kind of weightlessness that set him apart in a world where strength was everything. There was something honest in his eyes—something untouched by ambition or pride.

As they drank quietly, Tadanaka asked, "Did Father tell you anything?"

Yasaze shook his head. "No. Just sent a guard with a message for you. He didn't say anything else."

Tadanaka set his cup down and stared through the open doorway. The forest below was quiet, the wind weaving softly through the branches.

They finished their tea and stepped outside. The path to Toukan Castle wound through tall trees and narrow ridges. Yasaze walked just behind, quiet as always. Tadanaka said nothing, his focus fixed ahead as they made their way through the morning calm. Yasaze nodded at his brother, and they parted ways.

The gates of Toukan Castle opened without hesitation as Tadanaka Toukan approached. The guards recognized him instantly, stepping aside with quiet respect as he passed into the wide, stone-lined court-yard. Though this path was familiar to him, something about today felt heavier—less routine, more intentional. He moved swiftly from habit, knowing that when his father summoned him, it was never without purpose.

He entered the castle's main hall and found Yuuta Toukan, his father, the ruler of Alard, standing beneath a wide, open window. Light poured through the slats of carved wood, casting long, angled shadows across the floor. Yuuta stood motionless, hands behind his back, his presence calm but unmistakably commanding.

Tadanaka dropped to one knee. "Father."

Yuuta turned slightly, offering the briefest nod. "Stand. Walk with me."

No further explanation followed. Tadanaka rose and joined him without hesitation as they moved through the corridor and out a side entrance that led directly into the woods behind the castle. These walks weren't uncommon, but they were always deliberate—reserved for conversations requiring privacy, free from walls and ears.

The woods behind the castle stretched wide and silent. Tall trees arched overhead, their branches weaving a shifting canopy that filtered the light into golden fragments along the forest floor. The pair's footsteps crunched softly along the dirt path, the rhythm of their pace matching the rustle of the wind through the leaves.

"I hear the Gochuu have been deployed again," Yuuta said after a long silence, his eyes looking straight ahead.

"Yes," Tadanaka replied evenly. "There were reports of Mutants along the outer borders. I sent the Members in pairs to cover different sectors. I remained behind in case you needed me."

Yuuta made a quiet sound of acknowledgment, neither approving nor disapproving, but reflective. "You've learned to accurately read the situation. That instinct will serve you well."

They walked a little further before his father spoke again. "And your training?"

"I've made adjustments. I've been pushing my limits—longer hours, deeper focus on Reiki concentration. My speed's improving, but I know it's still not where it needs to be."

There was a pause as Yuuta considered his son's words, then spoke with the clarity of someone who measured praise carefully. "You're stronger than most, Tadanaka. That much is clear. But you want more, don't you?"

Tadanaka didn't hesitate. "I do."

He glanced toward his father briefly, then added, "I want to be strong enough to join the Nokuba...under Ryoze's command."

For a moment, Yuuta said nothing. The breeze moved gently through the branches above them as they walked deeper into the trees. When he finally responded, his voice was even.

"That path won't open easily. You know that. The Nokuba aren't chosen by blood, and your brother didn't reach that rank because of his name. He earned it—through pain, through discipline, through loss."

"I understand," Tadanaka said, his voice quieter now but steady. "That's why I want to earn it the same way."

Yuuta gave a slow nod, the faintest sign of approval touching his features. "Then keep pushing forward. Keep proving yourself. If your goal is to stand beside your brother, I won't stand in your way. I'll support you—but your strength must speak for itself."

"Understood," Tadanaka replied, lowering his head slightly with gratitude.

As the two men continued walking, unaware of how exposed they had become in the stillness of the forest, another presence followed behind.

Kume moved with the precision of someone trained to disappear. Her steps were soundless, her breath light, and her body kept low as she shadowed their path. Every tree, every patch of overgrowth became a point of concealment. She tracked Yuuta's pace more than Tadanaka's—her focus narrowed, fixed on the one man she had vowed to strike.

The opportunity was rare. She knew it. An unguarded walk through the forest, no entourage, no castle walls to shield him—only space and timing stood between her and the chance she had waited for. Yet the moment had to be perfect. A misstep would mean not only failure, but death.

So she stayed hidden, her eyes locked on her target, her every motion calculated with ruthless patience.

For several long moments, there was only the soft rhythm of footsteps along the wooded trail—Yuuta and Tadanaka moving in quiet conversation beneath the filtered light of the canopy. The wind shifted gently, brushing through the branches overhead. Everything seemed calm. Peaceful. Routine.

Then it happened.

Without a sound, Kume broke from the treeline.

Her eyes were locked on Yuuta, every muscle in her body surging with focus as she unleashed the Reiki she had been holding back. It built rapidly—light crackling at her fingertips, her blade drawn in one smooth, deliberate motion. In a single burst, she closed the distance with frightening speed, her presence breaking through the calm like lightning through still skies.

The blade struck.

Steel pierced cloth, skin, and bone as Kume's sword drove straight into Yuuta's chest.

His breath caught. A quiet grunt escaped his lips as he staggered back, falling to one knee as blood bloomed across his robes. The world seemed to freeze.

"Father!" Tadanaka cried out, his voice hoarse and raw. He rushed to his side, eyes wide with panic, barely processing what he had just seen. "Are you alright?" His hands hovered near his father, torn between helping him and turning to face the attacker.

But Kume was already standing there—just a few paces away—her chest rising and falling with uneven breath, her expression unreadable. The strike had landed. The plan had worked. She had done it. She had wounded the ruler of Alard.

For a moment, she felt triumph.

But it didn't last.

As she locked eyes with Tadanaka, her body tensed. She could feel his energy rising—his Reiki building like a storm behind his eyes. The ground beneath him stirred faintly with the pressure of it. His hands trembled with fury. His gaze burned into her like fire across dry grass, and for the first time in years, Kume hesitated.

She had planned to flee. She knew this was never meant to be a drawn-out fight. Hit, escape, disappear. That was the mission. But now—under Tadanaka's glare—her body refused to move. Her legs stayed rooted. Her heart pounded in her ears.

He took a step forward, the air around him crackling with Reiki.

And then—

"Tadanaka." Yuuta's voice was low but firm. Tired but unyielding.

It cut through the air like a command far louder than it was. Tadanaka froze mid step. He turned to his father, still kneeling, blood dripping slowly from his chest, but his eyes as sharp and steady as ever.

"Stand down," Yuuta said, his voice calm despite the pain.

Tadanaka clenched his fists. His chest rose with heavy breath as his Reiki pulsed wildly beneath the surface. But he didn't move forward. Slowly, his energy began to settle.

Kume's knees nearly gave out as the pressure eased. She staggered back a half step, breath caught in her throat. Relief washed over her like a crashing tide, though her muscles still refused to relax fully.

Back at the temple, Gerad sat in the corner, his expression unreadable. He stared at the ground for a long moment, his eyes unmoving, as though trying to calculate the outcome of a plan already set in motion.

Across from him, Kuna paced restlessly. Her hands fidgeted with the loose threads of her cloak, her breaths shallow. Though she said nothing, her movements betrayed her unease.

"She's been gone too long," Gerad muttered at last, his voice low but clear. "If she failed, we'll need to be ready to adjust. We can't let this entire effort collapse because of one misstep."

Kuna stopped pacing and turned to him sharply, her voice laced with anger. "Don't talk like that. She's not going to fail."

Gerad lifted an eyebrow, not in mockery but in the steady, unflinching manner of someone who had seen too many things go wrong. "Hope doesn't make plans. Caution does. We need a backup—"

"We don't need a backup," Kuna snapped, cutting him off. "My sister...she knows what she's doing. She's stronger than you think. She'll make it back."

Her words echoed in the empty chamber, bouncing between stone and silence. Gerad didn't respond right away. He watched her for a long moment, then slowly shifted his gaze toward the temple door.

"If she succeeds, everything changes," he said softly. "And if she doesn't...everything still does."

Kuna said nothing. She only turned her eyes to the darkness beyond the doorway, silently willing her sister to return—alive, victorious, and whole.

Back in the woods, the silence that followed the attack lingered like a heavy fog. Yuuta Toukan, still kneeling with a blade buried deep in his chest, slowly began to move. With the same calm that had marked his every step, he reached up and gripped the hilt of the weapon. Without flinching, he pulled it free in one clean motion. The metal slid from his body with a quiet, wet sound, darkened with blood—yet not a hint of weakness followed in his breath or posture.

He rose to his feet, tall and steady, the blade now resting in his hand like it had never belonged to the one who wielded it against him. The wound was real, the blood was real—but Yuuta stood as if he hadn't been struck at all.

Kume stared in stunned disbelief.

She had always known Yuuta Toukan wasn't someone who would fall easily. He was powerful—so much so that even rumors of his strength fell short of the truth. But for him to react like this? To rise as though the blade had never touched him?

She couldn't move. Her hands trembled, her thoughts racing too fast to process. Then, suddenly, another memory pushed its way into her awareness—one she had ignored in the chaos.

Just before the moment of impact, when she had burst from the trees and rushed toward him, blade drawn and Reiki burning bright, he had turned his head—not in surprise, but with calm certainty. He had looked directly at her.

And he had smiled.

It wasn't a smirk. It wasn't mockery. It was the expression of someone who had known she was there all along. A quiet, knowing acknowledgment.

He let me stab him.

The thought hit her harder than the realization that she had failed to kill him. *He could have stopped me. He could have moved, or blocked it, or simply vanished before I reached him. But he didn't.*

Why?

Was it pity? A test? Was there something more?

Questions flooded her mind, drowning her in a confusion she wasn't prepared for. She had awaited this chance for years—dreamed of it, trained for it—and now that the moment had come and passed, nothing made sense.

And then Yuuta spoke.

His voice was calm, low, and unwavering—like wind passing gently through tall grass.

"Settle yourself," he said, his eyes meeting hers without judgment. "You won't be harmed."

The words didn't carry threat or challenge. There was no show of dominance, no intent to strike back. Just that quiet, commanding certainty that made it clear: He was still in control.

Kume didn't know how to respond. Her body remained tense, her Reiki still pulsing faintly around her, but her resolve had begun to crumble.

Tadanaka stood a few paces behind his father, his body still tense, fists clenched tightly at his sides. The sight of Yuuta bleeding—no matter how composed his father appeared—had ignited something deep within him. His Reiki had calmed under Yuuta's command, but his fury had not vanished. It simmered beneath the surface, restrained only by discipline and respect.

He looked toward Kume, his glare sharp and unrelenting.

"What she did, is unacceptable. That kind of act cannot be overlooked or forgiven, even for a moment," he said, his voice raised with anger he no longer cared to conceal.

His eyes returned to his father, jaw tight with emotion.

"Father, give me permission," he said, each word deliberate and heavy with conviction. "Let me strike her down now, and end this disgrace before it spreads further."

The silence that followed was dense, pierced only by the sound of wind shifting lightly through the trees.

Yuuta, still standing tall despite the blood on his robes and the open wound in his chest, turned his head toward his son with a measured slowness. His expression, calm just moments before, darkened into something sharper, colder.

His gaze locked with Tadanaka's with a gravity that made Tadanaka immediately fall silent.

"I said, no harm will come to her." Yuuta spoke, his tone low but filled with finality.

The authority in his voice was absolute. There was no room left for argument, no space for protest. It wasn't a suggestion—it was an order.

Tadanaka held his father's gaze for a moment longer, then lowered his eyes. He bowed slowly, his pride still raw but his loyalty unshaken.

"Yes, Father," he said through clenched teeth.

He straightened without another word. The conflict still burned behind his eyes, but he would not disobey.

Yuuta took a slow step forward, his hand still loosely holding the bloodied blade that had pierced his own chest moments earlier. Though his wound remained, his posture was unshaken, his voice calm. His eyes settled on Kume, who now stood rigid and pale, yet unyielding.

He stopped only a few feet from her, looking at her with the steady presence of a man who had seen countless faces, read countless intentions, and now stood before one more.

"Tell me," he said, his voice firm yet composed, "what made you raise your blade against me?"

CHAPTER FOUR
She Who Struck the Ruler

Kume met his gaze without flinching. Her eyes, though cold and focused, held something deeper beneath the surface—something sharper than rage, something older than vengeance. There was no tremble in her stance, only the flicker of dark resolve behind her expression.

A bitter smirk pulled at the corner of her mouth. There was pain there. Pain that had never fully healed, and maybe never would.

"You really want to know?" she said, voice low and heavy with venom. "You—Yuuta Toukan, leader of this so-called peaceful land—you gave the order."

Yuuta's eyes narrowed, just slightly.

Kume continued, her voice hardening with every word.

"You ordered your Reiki warriors to destroy Joman Village. You thought it was being run by Mutahawls. You thought it had been taken over. So you sent warriors to wipe it from the map—without confirming anything, without asking questions, without knowing the truth."

Her breathing quickened, her fists clenched at her sides.

"You sent them to kill everyone. My parents. My grandparents. The elders. The children."

Her voice cracked slightly as the weight of memory returned like a blade pressing against her throat. She stared into Yuuta's face, searching for any sign of guilt, any flicker of doubt or regret—but found none. And that made the anger in her chest burn hotter.

Her hands curled into fists at her sides. Her body shook—not with fear, but with the fury of memories she could never erase.

"I wasn't there when it happened," she said, her voice dropping lower. "My sister and I...we were out training in the woods that day, just beyond the ridge. We weren't far. It was supposed to be a short session. Just a few hours."

She looked up at Yuuta, her eyes glistening with tears, but filled with rage all the same.

"When we came back, everything was already gone. The village was in ashes.

"There were bodies in the streets. My parents, my grandparents...all of them. Dead. The people we grew up with...scattered and burned."

Her breath trembled now, as her composure slipped just enough to show the wound beneath it.

"You took everything from us," she hissed. "And it wasn't a battle. It wasn't a war. It was a massacre—one you ordered."

She stared straight into Yuuta's eyes as her voice cracked and rose, raw and shaking.

"What do you have to say about that, Yuuta Toukan?" she screamed, the name leaving her lips like a curse. "What do you say to the girl who watched her entire village burn to the ground because of you?"

Yuuta remained still, his expression unwavering as he held Kume's fiery gaze. The raw anger in her voice didn't seem to shake him, nor did the accusation behind her words provoke a visible reaction. He simply looked at her—calm, composed, and resolute.

"I never gave an order to attack Joman Village," he said, his tone firm but even, every word delivered with quiet clarity, as if laying down an undeniable truth.

But Kume didn't let him finish.

Her rage surged again, cutting through his words like a blade. "Don't lie to me!" she shouted, her voice cracking as it rose. "Don't you dare stand there and pretend your hands aren't stained with the blood of my people!"

Yuuta's face did not change. He didn't flinch. He didn't argue. But beside him, the restraint in Tadanaka was quickly wearing thin.

The moment Kume raised her voice again, Tadanaka stepped forward, his eyes sharp with fury. He had held back as long as he could, out of respect for his father's presence and decisions, but her defiance—the way she spoke to Yuuta as though he were nothing more than a common criminal—had crossed a line.

"That's enough," Tadanaka said, his voice low but laced with threat. "You will watch your tone when you speak to my father. Another outburst like that, and I won't need permission to put an end to your life myself."

His hand hovered near his weapon, not drawn yet, but close.

But before Kume could respond, Yuuta lifted a hand slightly, a quiet signal that carried the weight of command far greater than any shout.

"Don't interfere," he said, his voice steady as ever, addressing his son without looking away from Kume. "This conversation is between her and me."

Tadanaka didn't speak again. He stepped back, jaw clenched, the fire still burning in his eyes. But he obeyed.

Then, almost as if a realization had clicked into place, a faint smile touched the corner of Yuuta's lips. It wasn't mocking, nor was it triumphant—it was the expression of a man who had finally uncovered something hidden beneath the surface.

Yuuta stepped forward calmly. Raising his hand with intent, he struck Kume lightly on the side of the head with the edge of his palm. The movement was gentle in appearance, but his control over his Reiki was so precise that even the softest strike caused her knees to buckle instantly. Her eyes fluttered as she lost consciousness, collapsing forward without resistance. Yuuta caught her before she hit the ground.

Lowering her gently to the earth, he placed one hand over her chest and the other at her side. His palms began to glow faintly, the flow of his Reiki moving in deliberate pulses. It wasn't an attack—it was something more refined, something inward. His energy pushed through her body, not to harm her, but to reveal something buried inside.

A moment later, something unnatural stirred beneath her skin.

From beneath her collarbone, a small black leech began to slither outward, writhing as it was forced from her body by the force of Yuuta's Reiki. It twisted violently, as though resisting, but it couldn't stay hidden any longer. The parasite was exposed—its presence unnatural, its energy dark and corrupted.

Tadanaka, who had been standing still but alert, took a cautious step forward, his expression shifting from confusion to alarm.

"What is that?" he asked, his voice low but urgent. "What's going on?"

Yuuta didn't look up as he focused on suppressing the creature, his hands still glowing faintly as he kept the Reiki flowing to neutralize its influence. His tone remained calm, but his words were heavy.

"She was being used," he said, watching the leech as it twitched and slowly dissolved beneath the force of his energy. "This isn't her hatred. It was planted inside her. A Mutahawl must have placed this leech in her body and used it to twist her memories—to turn her pain into a weapon."

Tadanaka's eyes narrowed, glancing from his father to Kume, then to the now-still creature lying beside her motionless body.

As the last traces of the leech dissolved beneath the pressure of Yuuta's Reiki, he remained kneeling beside Kume's unconscious form, his hand still resting gently over her chest as if to ensure whatever influence had taken root in her was now completely gone. He looked down at her face, and though she had tried to take his life only moments ago, there was no anger in his expression— only a quiet sorrow.

Yuuta had seen many forms of manipulation before. He had faced hatred in countless forms—some born from ambition, others from loss—but the kind forged through false memory was something far crueler. What had been done to this girl was not just an attack on the body, but on her sense of self. She had lived with pain that did not belong to her, carried a vengeance built on illusions that had been forced into her mind by something dark and deliberate.

He exhaled quietly, the weight of the moment heavy in his chest, and turned his gaze toward his son, who still stood nearby—tense, alert, and silent.

"Tadanaka," Yuuta said, his voice steady but more subdued than before. "Take her back with you to the Gochuu base."

Tadanaka looked at him, his expression unreadable, but he didn't question the order.

"She'll need time," Yuuta continued. "Time to rest, to recover...and to understand the truth when she's ready to hear it. I want you to look after her for a while. Until then, she is not to be treated as an enemy."

Tadanaka gave a slow, respectful nod, the fire in his eyes now tempered with understanding. "I'll keep her safe."

Yuuta rose slowly to his feet, the blood on his robes already drying, and watched as his son gently lifted Kume into his arms, cradling her as though she were a wounded ally rather than a would-be assassin.

Meanwhile, at the abandoned temple, Gerad sat hunched in thought, though his mind was clearly far from the walls around him.

It had been too long.

The forest should have echoed with Kume's return by now—either in victory or urgency—but instead, there was only silence. Something about it felt wrong. Unnatural. His instincts, honed by years of surviving on darkness and deception, twisted uncomfortably in his gut.

He stood slowly, eyes narrowing, and turned toward Kuna, who had been pacing near the edge of the temple, growing more anxious by the minute.

"Something isn't right," Gerad snapped. "Too much time has passed. Go find her."

Kuna's brows lifted in concern, but she didn't hesitate.

"Find her," he repeated, "and return to me with what you learn. If something's happened, I need to know exactly what."

Kuna gave a firm nod, then turned and rushed into the woods, her cloak catching the wind as she vanished into the treeline, heading toward the last known path her sister had taken.

Back at the Gochuu base, soft light slipped through wooden slats as Kume slowly woke. The room was quiet, unfamiliar, and neatly kept, with weapons and scrolls arranged with careful precision. As she sat up, she realized she was alone. Her body still ached faintly, and the weight of everything that had happened pressed against her thoughts.

She didn't know where she was, but she could sense she was safe—for now.

SURU

In the main hall, the remaining Members of the Gochuu had just returned from their missions and stood before Tadanaka. Suru, silent as always, remained still and observant. Miji, visibly irritated by something minor, crossed his arms with a scowl. Satora, the most energetic of the three, leaned casually with a half-grin, already making light of the situation in her usual playful tone.

MIJI   SATORA

Tadanaka listened to their reports, but before he could speak, footsteps approached from the corridor.

Kume entered the hall.

She walked with purpose, her eyes scanning the unfamiliar faces only briefly before settling on Tadanaka. He stepped forward to greet her and turned to his team.

"This is Kume," he said calmly. "She'll be staying with us."

The others nodded, but Kume barely acknowledged them. Her voice cut through the room, steady and direct.

"I don't care who they are. Tell me what happened."

Tadanaka stepped forward and, with a calm and measured voice, told Kume that he would explain everything she wanted to know, but that they should speak in the open air of the Gochuu's training grounds.

Without protest, Kume gave a slight nod, and the group made their way through the base's winding corridors, eventually stepping outside into the wide, open courtyard surrounded by stone paths and wooden targets weathered by years of use.

The Gochuu training field stretched wide beneath the fading sky, a space designed for movement, sparring, and concentration. The soft sound of the wind moving through the trees along the outer edge accompanied their footsteps as they entered the clearing. The Members of the Gochuu followed at a short distance, silent but watchful, each sensing that this conversation was not just for Kume's sake—but for theirs as well.

As they came to a stop near the center of the field, Tadanaka, ever the composed leader, tried to soften the moment. He gestured lightly toward the field, offering Kume a brief glance and asked, not without sincerity, "What do you think of the training grounds? You'll be seeing quite a bit of them while you're here."

Kume, however, didn't return the tone. Her expression unshifting, her eyes didn't move to admire the space around her. She stood firm, replying in a cool and unbending voice.

"I'm not here to admire anything," she said, cutting straight through the attempt at conversation. "I want you to stop dancing around it and tell me what happened. I can't remember anything after what I thought I did, and I need the truth—not distractions."

Her words, though not hostile, carried enough edge to draw a reaction from behind.

Miji, already irritated from earlier, stepped forward with a glare, unable to restrain himself any longer. His tone was sharp and full of scorn.

"Who the hell does she think she is, talking to Captain Tadanaka like that? Some nobody stumbles in here, forgets who she is, and suddenly she's giving orders?"

The moment stretched with tension, but Tadanaka raised a hand gently before anyone else could speak. His voice remained calm, steady, and in control.

"It's alright, Miji," he said, glancing back over his shoulder. " She has the right to ask."

Tadanaka stood in the center of the training field, his posture straight, his voice calm yet firm as he began to recount the truth—every detail he had witnessed, every piece his father had revealed.

He explained the influence of the leech, how it had been implanted in Kume by a Mutahawl, how it had twisted her memories and poisoned her thoughts. He told her that the hatred she had felt—the drive that had led her to attempt to kill his father—had not truly been hers, but something that had been forced upon her. He did not embellish or hold anything back. There was no need. The truth alone was heavy enough.

As he spoke, the other Members of the Gochuu listened in silence, each of them processing the weight of what they were hearing. Their expressions were varied—Suru stood still, as unreadable as ever, offering no reaction beyond a subtle narrowing of his eyes.

Satora, usually so quick to speak or lighten the mood, had grown noticeably quiet, her gaze shifting between Kume and Tadanaka.

Miji, however, could not mask his disbelief or his rising frustration.

When Tadanaka explained that Kume had, under manipulation, attacked Yuuta Toukan, a visible wave of shock passed through them. The thought that someone had dared to raise a weapon against the ruler of Alard—a man revered by all of them—was nearly unthinkable. The idea that she had done so and now stood here, among them, under their captain's protection, was more than some of them could easily accept.

Kume lowered her head as fragments of her memory began returning. The sounds, the flashes of movement, the face of Yuuta as she struck him—all of it came back in uneven pieces. Her eyes narrowed and she took a step forward, her voice rising with a fresh swell of emotion.

"No," she said, her tone turning sharp. "You're lying to me. Both of you— Yuuta, and now you—you're trying to make me doubt myself. I know what I saw, I know what I felt, and I want to speak to him directly. I won't accept this unless I hear it from his mouth."

Her demand rang out across the field, and for a heartbeat, no one moved.

Then, without warning, Miji snapped.

He rushed forward, faster than anyone expected, his Reiki flaring in anger. Kume barely had time to react before he tackled her hard to the ground, pinning her beneath him with the weight of his fury. The edge of his blade pressed firmly against her neck, his face twisted with rage.

"You don't get to speak his name like that," he growled, his voice shaking. "You think you can come here, threaten Master Yuuta, insult Captain Tadanaka, and then demand answers? If you keep running your mouth, I'll slit your throat and save everyone the trouble."

"Miji, stand down!" Tadanaka's voice rang out across the field, filled with authority and rising anger. He stepped forward quickly, his presence commanding the attention of everyone present.

But Miji didn't move.

His grip on the blade didn't ease, and his eyes remained locked on Kume. Whatever respect he had for his captain was being smothered by something deeper—pure, unrelenting fury. His loyalty to Yuuta had been shaken, and his temper, already known for its volatility, now flared beyond reason.

From several paces away, Tadanaka took a firm step forward, his voice calm but laced with warning. "Don't do anything reckless, Miji. This isn't the way."

His words were clear, but they barely reached Miji through the haze of emotion. Kume's eyes met his without fear, her jaw clenched as she responded in a low, steady tone. "If you don't get off me right now...I'll kill you."

Her threat wasn't shouted. It wasn't bluster. It was spoken with the kind of quiet conviction that made it clear she meant every word.

Miji blinked—and then, unexpectedly, he started laughing.

The sound was sharp, almost manic, echoing across the training field. He pulled the blade back and stepped away from her, allowing her to rise. His laughter continued as he sheathed his sword and stretched his arms slightly, rolling his shoulders as if preparing for a warm-up.

"I'd love to see you try," he said, his grin wide, though his eyes remained serious. "Come on then. Show me what you've got."

With that, he took a step back and exhaled slowly. The air around him shifted as he released his Reiki into the open. It rushed out in a forceful wave, swirling around him in sharp gusts that stirred the dust beneath his feet and sent a ripple through the field.

Kume stood still for a moment, her gaze narrowing as she felt the pressure of his energy. It was raw and aggressive—hot-headed and unstable, much like the boy himself. Still, she didn't back down. Instead, she drew in a breath, spread her stance, and released her own Reiki in response.

The air changed again.

Her energy rolled forward in a pulse of clean, focused force. It didn't roar like Miji's—it hummed, steady and sharp, like a blade drawn just before the strike. Miji, despite his arrogance, immediately felt the shift in weight. His smirk faded just slightly, the tensing of his muscles giving away what his mouth didn't say.

He hadn't expected her to be this strong.

Several paces away, Suru turned slightly toward Tadanaka, his expression as calm as ever. His voice, quiet and reserved, carried easily across the space. "Shall I intervene, Captain?"

Tadanaka didn't answer right away. He watched the two across the field—the way their Reiki danced in opposition, the way neither one showed a hint of hesitation. For a few moments he said nothing, his arms crossed as he observed them carefully.

Then, finally, he spoke.

"No," he said. "Let them go on. I want to see what Kume is really capable of."

Kume's eyes locked onto Miji, and without hesitation, she reached for her sword. In one swift, practiced motion, she drew the blade and dashed forward, her body propelled by focused Reiki and a clear intent to meet his challenge head-on. The air between them split with the force of her movement, and in seconds she was upon him.

Miji met her without flinching. He pivoted with sharp reflexes, drawing his own weapon just in time to parry her first strike. The sound of metal clashing against metal rang out across the training field, and with it, the duel truly began. Each blow exchanged was fast, deliberate, and filled with purpose. The two moved like seasoned opponents, not strangers. Every step, every slash, every dodge was executed with precision.

The Members of the Gochuu stood in a loose circle around them, none daring to interrupt. Even Satora, whose usual energy had quieted, watched in awe as the battle unfolded. Suru remained unreadable, though his gaze never left the fighters. The intensity of the clash had captured them all.

As the minutes passed, it became increasingly clear that both Kume and Miji were holding nothing back. Though Miji was younger and quicker to anger, his combat instinct was undeniable, and his skill with a blade was matched by very few.

But Kume, though less familiar to them, showed a level of focus and adaptability that gave her a steady edge. Her movements grew more fluid with each exchange, as if she were reading Miji's style in real time and adjusting to every opening.

They paused for a brief moment, weapons clashing and locking at the midpoint between them. Their eyes met, and for the first time, both of them saw it—the unspoken acknowledgment that they had underestimated each other.

Then Kume broke the lock, spun low, and moved in for what would have been the final strike. Her blade arced forward, aimed with precision and force.

But just before it could land, Tadanaka stepped in.

His body moved like a gust of wind, swift and exact, and with a single motion, he placed himself between the two. His arm caught Kume's wrist with firm control, halting the blade inches before it could reach its mark.

"That's enough," he said, his voice even and commanding, his eyes shifting between the two fighters.

The tension broke in an instant. Kume stepped back, lowering her weapon, her breathing still heavy. Miji didn't speak, but he relaxed his stance and slowly sheathed his blade.

As the dust settled across the training field and the final tension from the duel faded into the wind, Tadanaka stepped closer to Kume, his eyes still slightly wide with admiration. There was no doubt in his expression—he was impressed by her technique, composure, and instinct, as well as the way she had held her own against one of his best.

"You're a hell of a fighter," he said with a genuine nod. "Where did you learn to move like that?"

Kume lowered her sword slowly and slid it back into its sheath, her breath still steady from the exchange. She looked up at him, her voice calm and clear, though there was a flicker of emotion behind her words.

"I started training when I was very young," she said. "But after my family was killed...I stopped training for fun and started training for revenge. Every strike, every breath, every hour I spent sharpening my skills—was for them. I made myself a promise that I'd avenge my family."

Tadanaka listened closely, and for a moment, said nothing. Then a small smile touched his lips, and he gave a firm nod of approval.

"You're tough," he said simply. "Stronger than most. That wasn't just skill— that was heart."

Before Kume could respond, Satora, who had been standing off to the side with an amused look on her face, suddenly laughed and pointed toward Miji, who was still quietly adjusting the strap of his blade.

"Well," she said with a grin, "looks like our hot-headed champ just got beaten by a girl. That's going in the record books."

Miji turned sharply, his scowl returning almost instantly. He opened his mouth to respond but caught himself, glanced at Kume, and then shook his head with a short exhale. After a moment, he walked up to her with his hands loosely at his sides, his expression more composed.

"You're good," he said, his tone more respectful than before. "I've got to give it to you. That was a solid fight."

Kume gave him a small nod, her tone just as even. "It was. I haven't had one like that in a while. Thanks."

As the tension between them eased, Satora couldn't resist chiming in again, this time nudging Miji lightly with her elbow. "I'm just saying, Miji, next time maybe try fighting with your eyes open."

The jab earned a collective laugh from the group. Even Kume, who hadn't smiled once since arriving at the base, let out a soft laugh that came almost by surprise. For the first time, the sharp edge of her presence began to ease.

CHAPTER FIVE
Her Reiki was Enough

Kume suddenly dropped to her knees, her sword slipping from her grasp as she let out a piercing scream that echoed through the air. Her hands gripped at her chest, her breath caught somewhere between her lungs and her throat. Her eyes, wide with terror, darted across the space around her, though they couldn't seem to focus on anything. She clawed at the ground, her voice rising in panic.

"W-What is this?!" she gasped, barely able to speak. "This...this Reiki—what is it?! I can't move...I can't breathe...!"

She tried to stand but collapsed again, trembling uncontrollably. The fear in her voice was unlike anything the Gochuu had heard from her. It wasn't pain that overtook her—it was sheer, suffocating terror. She began muttering to herself, her words frantic and disjointed.

"I've never felt anything like this before. It's too strong...too cold. Is this even possible?"

Tadanaka was the first to move. He rushed to her side, dropping to one knee and gripping her shoulders, trying to steady her. "Kume, what's wrong? Talk to me—what's happening?!"

But she couldn't respond. Her voice was lost, replaced by shallow, panicked gasps as her body trembled under an invisible pressure that none of them could yet understand.

The rest of the Gochuu looked around, alarmed. Suru narrowed his eyes, Satora's smile vanished, and Miji stepped forward with his hand hovering over his sword.

None of them could explain what was happening.

Then they felt it too.

A presence—dense, cold, suffocating—was moving toward them. It wasn't visible yet, but the weight of the approaching energy made the air itself feel thick. The earth beneath their feet seemed to resist motion, and the wind itself fell silent.

"Someone's coming," Satora said quietly, her voice no longer playful.

"Who is it?!" Tadanaka shouted toward the edge of the field.

And then his expression shifted.

His confidence, steady until now, gave way to something unfamiliar—fear.

His mouth barely moved as the words fell from him. "This is bad... This is really bad...It's Lord Shita."

SHITA TOUKAN

The moment her name left his lips, the remaining Gochuu Members froze in place. Not a single one dared to speak. Their instincts told them what their bodies already knew—this was not someone to be taken lightly.

From the shadows, a woman emerged, her steps slow but deliberate. Shita Toukan, her expression unreadable, walked into the field with the poise of someone who never needed to raise her voice to command fear. A black eyepatch bearing the Toukan crest covered her left eye—an ever-present reminder of both what she'd endured and what she was capable of. Her remaining eye scanned the group with sharp precision, settling coldly on Kume, who lay writhing at the center.

"Where is the damn kid who stabbed Master Yuuta?" she asked, her tone flat and ice-cold.

None of the Gochuu answered. Not Suru, not Miji, not even Satora—they remained rooted where they stood, silent, as if speaking might provoke her further.

Shita began walking toward Kume, the Reiki around her so intense that even without moving a muscle, she was forcing everyone to feel it in their bones. Tadanaka immediately stepped into her path and bowed, his voice calm but desperate.

"Please, don't harm her. She's under my protection."

But Shita didn't stop. She walked straight past him without so much as a glance, brushing him aside with only the pressure of her presence. Her voice, low and razor-sharp, left no room for debate.

"Shut up, kid. I'll kill you next if you get in my way."

Tadanaka stepped back, stunned. Still, he tried again. "I'm begging you—just wait. Please listen."

But she didn't.

Shita now stood directly over Kume, who lay on the ground, paralyzed by the sheer force of Shita's Reiki. Her mouth opened slightly, but no sound came out. Her body wouldn't respond—she couldn't move, couldn't speak. Every nerve inside her screamed, but her limbs had abandoned her.

Shita slowly reached for the sword at her side, her voice like a dagger in the cold.

"So this is the weakling who thought it was a good idea to attack Master Yuuta?" she said with quiet disgust.

She unsheathed her blade, raising it above Kume, her grip steady.

But before the strike could fall, Tadanaka shouted louder than before, his voice cutting through the weight of Shita's Reiki.

"Wait! It was Master Yuuta's order!" he cried. "He told me himself—he said she was to be left alive and placed under my protection!"

Shita stopped mid-motion.

She turned her head slowly toward him, her eyes sharp and suspicious. "Is that what you're saying?" she asked coldly. "Are you telling me that was Master Yuuta's direct command?"

Tadanaka nodded quickly, the sincerity in his voice unshakable. "Yes. I swear it."

For a long moment, Shita didn't speak. Then, with a sigh that seemed to release the pressure from the entire field, she concealed her Reiki. The suffocating weight lifted. Kume gasped as air filled her lungs again, her body finally responding to her will.

Shita turned from her, walking past Tadanaka once more. As she did, she stopped just beside him, casting him a frigid glare over her shoulder.

"If I find out you lied to me, I'll beat your ass myself," she said without a hint of humor.

With that, she walked away, her figure fading back into the shadows as silently as she had arrived.

The moment she was gone; the Gochuu Members finally moved. They exhaled as if they had been holding their breath the entire time. Tadanaka immediately knelt beside Kume, checking her breathing as the others gathered close.

"Who was that?" Kume asked, her voice barely more than a whisper.

Tadanaka looked her in the eyes and answered, his voice serious. "That was Lord Shita."

Kume's expression changed instantly, her lips parting as her eyes widened in disbelief.

"You know her?" Tadanaka asked.

"You mean Shita Toukan…The Ice Lord? Second in command and Master Yuuta's right hand? Everyone's heard of her. Of course I know that name," Kume replied.

Tadanaka gave a small nod. The name alone had spoken volumes.

CHAPTER SIX
Bring Her Back Dead

It was late into the night, and the Gochuu base had long since fallen into silence. The stars hung dimly above the training field, their faint glow casting silver outlines across the stone and dirt. The cool, still air carried the quiet of a land momentarily at peace.

Kume, restless and unable to sleep, stepped out into the open, hoping that the fresh air might calm her thoughts. Her quiet footsteps barely disturbed the earth beneath her as she made her way toward the center of the field.

To her surprise, she wasn't alone.

Tadanaka was already there, seated near one of the practice posts with his arms draped loosely over his knees, his gaze lost somewhere in the distance. Although he didn't turn when she approached, his voice rose gently in the quiet.

"You couldn't sleep either, huh?"

Kume gave a small nod, lowering herself beside him with a soft but tired expression. For a few moments, neither spoke. The silence between them was not uncomfortable—it was shared, reflective, even comforting in its simplicity.

Eventually, Tadanaka glanced her way, his voice carrying the weight of sincerity. "I wanted to say I'm sorry about what happened earlier—with Shita," he said. "I know it was intense, and I know it might be hard to shake off, but...try not to take it personally."

He leaned back slightly, grinning. "You'd probably like her if you got to know her better. I mean, sure, she's terrifying...but she's loyal. If she respects you, she'll protect you with everything she has. Still, even if you hold a grudge, let's be honest—there's not much you could do about it. She's scary."

Kume let out a soft laugh, the tension in her shoulders easing. Tilting her head, she gave him a sideways glance.

"Do you think...I could talk to her?" she asked. "In the morning, maybe?"

Tadanaka turned to face her fully, his eyes widening as if he wasn't sure he had heard correctly.

"Talk to her?" he repeated, his tone exaggerated in disbelief. "After today?"

He blinked, shaking his head slowly while laughing under his breath. "Sure, go ahead. But if she cuts you down where you stand, don't come crying to me." Kume laughed along, the mood between them finally lightening. For a while, they continued talking beneath the stars with low, easy voices, like two people who had finally begun to understand each other.

Beyond the tree line, in the darkness of the woods just beyond the training field, a pair of eyes was watching them closely.

Kuna, hidden beneath the cover of night, observed their every word, her body still and silent as she took in everything—waiting for the right moment to return with what she had learned.

At Yuuta's castle the night was quiet, the halls lit by soft lantern light. Though vast and commanding, the castle held a calm stillness at its core—especially within the chamber where Yuuta Toukan awaited.

The doors slid open and Shita stepped through, her posture straight and unwavering. She crossed the room and dropped to one knee before him, her head bowed in respect.

"My Lord," she said. "About the girl—Kume. Is it true you gave permission for her to remain at the Gochuu base?"

Yuuta gave her a small nod. His voice, as always, was calm and clear.

"Yes. She's been through more than most could endure. Be kind to her, Shita."

There was no hesitation in her reply. "Understood," she said, her voice steady.

Yuuta studied her for a moment, then leaned back slightly. "And what of your mission?" he asked. "Did you find what you were looking for?"

Shita fell silent. For a second, she didn't speak; when she finally answered, the hesitation in her voice betrayed a rare moment of vulnerability.

"Not yet," she said quietly. "But I will continue at first light. I promise you— I'll find a way."

Her words were desperate—not in fear, but in sheer determination. Whatever she was searching for, it clearly mattered more than she allowed others to see.

Yuuta's expression softened. He stood and approached her, placing both hands gently on her shoulders. His tone was not commanding, but warm.

"Enough, Shita. You've done more than anyone could ask. Stay here for now. Rest. There's no need to rush."

Shita looked up as if about to object, but Yuuta gave her a small smile and added one final remark.

"That's an order."

The firmness in his voice, even when paired with kindness, made it clear he would not be swayed.

"...understood," Shita murmured, lowering her head once more. Her usually cold and sharp voice now carried something softer—something tired.

Kuna returned to the shadowed temple with urgency in her steps, the weight of what she had seen pressing heavily on her chest. The journey through the forest had been swift and silent, driven by the images still clinging to her mind— Kume standing beside Tadanaka Toukan, her expression compassionate, her posture relaxed, as if she belonged at the Gochuu base.

She found Gerad seated in the inner chamber, surrounded by the faint flicker of torchlight and the scent of damp stone. As she entered, his eyes lifted slightly but he said nothing, waiting for her to speak first.

"I saw her," Kuna said, not bothering with formality. "She was with Tadanaka, Lord Yuuta's son. But something was...different." Gerad remained silent, watching her closely.

"She didn't look like someone being held captive. She looked...comfortable. Her guard was down. I don't know what they've done to her, but we can't wait any longer. We need to act. We have to save her—before they take her from us."

For a moment, Gerad said nothing. His expression didn't change, but something in the stillness around him shifted. Slowly standing up with his hands clasped behind his back, he walked to the far side of the temple where the air was colder.

"She's being manipulated," he said finally, his calm voice betraying a sharp edge. "Whatever kindness they're showing her, it isn't real. They've twisted her thoughts, convinced her she's safe. But she's not one of them."

He raised his hand without another word, summoning several Mutahawls from the outer halls of the temple. Each of their lean, silent forms carried the unmistakable aura of Dark Reiki—a steady pressure that filled the room like a rising tide. These were not ordinary Mutants. They were Gerad's most trusted followers, each one dangerous, each one unwaveringly loyal.

Gerad turned to them, speaking with clear, deliberate authority.

"Your mission is simple," he said. "Go and eliminate Tadanaka Toukan and every one of his warriors. Retrieve Kume and bring her back here. Alive."

The Mutants nodded in mute acknowledgment, already preparing to depart. Although their steps were silent, their presence lingered like smoke.

As they neared the exit, Gerad raised his hand again. "Wait," he said quietly.

Kuna had already turned away, her attention drawn to something else within the temple. She didn't hear what followed.

Gerad lowered his voice, speaking to his Mutants alone. His tone shifted— quieter now, but edged with finality.

"If she resists...if she refuses to come back...you have permission to kill her. Do not waste time trying to convince her."

He said no more.

The Mutahawls bowed and disappeared into the darkness, their path set. Kuna remained unaware behind them, still clinging to the hope that this mission was about saving her sister.

The next morning, just as Kume and Tadanaka were preparing to leave the Gochuu base to meet with Shita, Tadanaka walked toward the main door and slid it open—only to stop in surprise at the sight waiting just outside. Standing there was his younger brother Yasaze; beside him, smiling brightly, was a little girl who wasted no time rushing forward.

"Hala!" Tadanaka called out excitedly as he knelt down to catch her in his arms. She jumped at him without hesitation, wrapping her arms around his neck as he lifted her effortlessly.

HALA

Hala—Tadanaka's niece, Ryoze's daughter—clung to him happily before pulling back just enough to study the girl standing beside him. Her expression turning curious, she pointed at Kume without skipping a beat.

"Is that your girlfriend?" she asked with complete seriousness.

Tadanaka laughed as he set her down, shaking his head while glancing briefly at Kume, who looked slightly caught off guard by the question. "No," he said with a grin, "she's just a new friend."

Yasaze stepped forward then, his tone gentle and his posture as calm as ever. "So, you're Kume?" he asked, offering a respectful nod.

Tadanaka stepped in to make the introduction properly. "Kume, this is my younger brother, Yasaze Toukan. Yasaze, this is Kume."

Kume returned the nod with polite acknowledgment.

Tadanaka returned his attention to them, eyebrow raised. "So, what brings you both here this early?"

Yasaze folded his hands behind his back and answered simply. "Hala wanted to visit you, and I didn't have the heart to say no."

Tadanaka smiled, preparing to explain that he and Kume were just heading to the main castle when Hala cut in before he could finish.

"I want to go into town!" she said, tugging at his sleeve. "You promised last time that you'd take me and buy me candy, and you never did!"

Caught off guard, Tadanaka looked from her to Yasaze, who was already smiling.

"You heard her," Yasaze said, clearly amused. "You know she's not going to let it go."

Tadanaka sighed, though the corners of his mouth curved into a reluctant smile. He looked down at Hala, who was staring up at him with her arms crossed, clearly waiting for an answer.

"Alright," he said, giving in. "Town it is."

Still, even with the lighthearted shift in plans, Tadanaka didn't forget the risks. He turned to call for Satora, knowing full well that even a quick visit into town involved dangers.

With Mutants still lurking out there, he wasn't about to take any chances—not with Hala by his side. Having another Member of the Gochuu present would better prepare them for anything unexpected.

And while the visit to the castle would have to wait a little longer, Tadanaka didn't mind. For now, Hala's smile made the detour feel like the right choice.

The group of five made their way into town, moving together through the main street as merchants and townsfolk began their usual morning routines. Tadanaka walked slightly ahead with Hala by his side, his eyes scanning the area while still managing to keep the tone of their outing light. Before they reached the town square, he knelt slightly and looked Hala in the eye.

"I want you to stay close to me at all times," he said firmly, though not unkindly. "Don't wander off, and don't step out of my sight. Understand?"

Hala nodded quickly, sensing the seriousness in his voice. When she unprotestingly reached for his hand, he gave her a small smile before standing upright again.

As they approached the restaurant area, Yasaze slowed his pace and turned slightly to the side. "I'll catch up with you in a little while," he said. "There's something I need to buy real quick." Without waiting for a reply, he turned down a side road and disappeared into the nearby shops.

The others continued on, soon finding a quiet place to sit. The restaurant was small but clean, with wooden benches and an open view of the street.

Tadanaka, Kume, Hala, and Satora settled around a table. After taking a quick look at the menu, Tadanaka signaled the server and ordered a round of food for everyone.

As they waited, Hala leaned on the table, swinging her feet and chatting with Satora, who had already started teasing her about how much candy she could eat in one day.

Meanwhile, not far from the restaurant, Yasaze entered a modest little bookstore tucked between two shops. The scent of paper and ink filled the room, and he took his time browsing through the shelves. Eventually, he stopped at a small corner where older titles were displayed. As he reached for a particular volume, he noticed someone standing just a few feet away, also scanning the selection.

SHIRO

A simply-dressed woman with a composed, thoughtful expression, had just picked up a book and was flipping through its pages.

"That's a great choice," Yasaze said, glancing over with a small nod. "I've read it before. I'd definitely recommend it."

The woman looked up, her expression softening. She studied the book for a moment, then nodded. "In that case, I'll take it," she said. She turned to the shop owner and placed it on the counter.

Yasaze watched her for a moment before speaking again. "I don't believe I've seen you around here before."

"I just arrived," she replied. "I'm new to the area."

She extended a hand with a polite smile. "My name is Shiro."

"Yasaze," he responded, shaking her hand gently.

They spoke for a few more minutes, mostly small talk about the town, the shop, and the weather. Shiro seemed kind, and eventually she glanced toward the door as if remembering she had somewhere else to be.

"It was nice meeting you," she said, offering a slight bow before turning to leave.

Yasaze nodded, returning the gesture. "You too."

He stayed for a few seconds longer, then made his way out of the store and walked back toward the restaurant where his brother and the others were waiting.

As the group made their way back from town, Hala was clinging to Tadanaka's back, her arms wrapped around his neck as she laughed softly, clearly enjoying the ride. Kume walked beside him, while Satora trailed just behind, keeping an eye on their surroundings. Yasaze walked ahead a short distance, his pace relaxed, still carrying the book he had picked up from the shop.

They were only a few minutes away from the castle gates when everything changed.

Six figures stepped out from the woods without warning, blocking their path from the front. The formerly peaceful dirt path had become a trap.

The mysterious group's energy was unmistakable—thick, dark, and heavy with malice.

Mutants.

Not hesitating for a second, Tadanaka immediately reached up, took Hala from his back, and turned to his brother. "Yasaze," he said quickly in a sharp yet controlled tone, "take her."

Yasaze stepped forward without hesitation, taking Hala and cradling her in his arms. The little girl didn't speak, sensing the sudden change in atmosphere. She remained still, her wide eyes darting from face to face.

Tadanaka turned to Satora next. "Stay close to them," he said firmly. "If things go wrong, you take them and run. Don't look back."

Satora gave a single nod, her playful demeanor gone in an instant, replaced by focus. She positioned herself beside Yasaze and scanned the area, already anticipating which direction a fight might come from.

The moment grew tense as the six Mutahawls stepped into view, surrounding Tadanaka, Kume, Yasaze, Hala, and Satora on the narrow path leading back to the castle.

Their sudden appearance had instantly shifted the atmosphere. The air, once filled with the sound of footsteps and faint laughter, now felt heavy with danger. Every movement from the attackers was dripping with intent.

One of the Mutants stepped forward, clearly the one in charge. His Dark Reiki crackled faintly in the air around him as he studied the group, a crooked smirk spreading across his face. His voice, though calm, was laced with cruel certainty.

"It's unfortunate," he said, almost mockingly. "But we'll have to kill you all.

"Don't worry—we'll make it quick."

He paused, his eyes sliding over to Kume with chilling focus.

"Except for you," he added. "You're coming with us."

The others froze. Kume's body tensed immediately, and though she didn't say a word, she already knew what this was. These weren't random attackers. This was deliberate. Gerad had sent them. He didn't trust her—or maybe he never had. Whatever reason he had for this mission, it was now unfolding right in front of her. But the others didn't know. To them, this was just another ambush.

Tadanaka stepped forward, his hand resting on the hilt of his weapon, his eyes never leaving the lead Mutant. "Who sent you?" he asked, his tone firm and commanding.

None of the Mutants answered. Their silence spoke volumes—then all at once, they lunged.

There was no time to speak. No time to warn. The fight had begun.

Tadanaka immediately released his Reiki, its force cracking through the air like a sudden gust of wind. The ground beneath his feet shifted with the pressure, several of the Mutants being briefly forced back by the intensity. But they weren't ordinary. Though his energy intimidated them, they didn't retreat. Surrounding him, their coordinated, efficient, and aggressive attacks came from multiple directions.

He fought back with everything he had. His strikes were clean, precise, and purposeful. But even for someone of his skill, the odds were brutal. There were six of them, each strong in their own right. He held his ground, but they clearly had the advantage in numbers, with their only goal to overwhelm and kill.

Just a few paces away, Satora stepped forward as she saw the situation growing worse, preparing to rush to her captain's aid. But Tadanaka, without turning, shouted over the noise of battle.

"Stay where you are! Don't leave Hala's side!"

Satora froze mid-step, torn between duty and instinct. Her fists clenched, but she obeyed. She moved closer to Yasaze and Hala, standing between them and the threat, ready to protect them if it came to that.

From behind her, Hala's voice rose in a shaky cry. "Uncle!"

Tadanaka glanced back for the briefest moment and forced a smile, even as he blocked another incoming strike. "I'm alright," he called out. "Stay close to Yasaze."

But the sound of battle wasn't the only thing rattling the group. Kume still hadn't moved.

She stood back, frozen, her expression torn between fear, guilt, and confusion.

She hadn't drawn her sword. Her body was tense, but not in preparation to fight. She was debating.

In her mind, everything was spinning. *Should I help them? Should I let Tadanaka die and go back to Gerad? What will happen if I fight them? What will happen if I don't?*

Hala shouted—her voice cutting through the clash of steel.

"Why are you just standing there, Kume?! Help my uncle!"

Kume's eyes snapped toward her. The words struck something deep in her chest. That voice...It didn't come from a warrior or a commander—it came from a child who still believed Kume could be trusted. That she was someone worth calling out to. That she was still on their side.

As Tadanaka fought off the relentless wave of attacks, he was holding back. Not because he lacked strength—but because Yasaze and Hala were still within range. If he unleashed his full power, the backlash of his Reiki could seriously hurt them. He was trying to win without risking the people behind him.

He managed to land a crushing blow to one of the Mutants, piercing the heart with a single precise strike. The Mutant collapsed instantly, unmoving. That was the only way to kill them—either the heart or the brain. Anything else, and they would keep coming.

But even as one went down, two others slipped past the fight and turned their eyes toward Hala.

Satora immediately intercepted the first. Sparks flying as they engaged, her movements sharp and unwavering. The second Mutant, however, slipped past her and sprinted directly toward Hala.

Tadanaka saw it the moment it happened. Shifting his entire body, he pushed off the ground and dashed toward Hala, ignoring the opening he left behind him.

He didn't care. He didn't think. His only thought was her.

He shouted her name with everything he had. "Hala!"

But he wasn't going to make it.

The Mutant was too fast, too close. He reached out, eyes wild, ready to strike.

Tadanaka's voice broke. "Please! Stop!"

And then—Kume moved.

Faster than the eye could follow, she rushed forward and threw herself between the Mutant and Hala. Her sword was out, her energy surging. She blocked the strike with the full force of her Reiki, her body lowered in a firm stance, protecting the girl behind her.

The Mutant glared down at her. "Move," he hissed. "Or I'll kill you too."

Kume didn't move. She stood her ground, eyes locked with his. "I'm not letting you touch her."

She turned her head just enough to look at Tadanaka. "You handle the others," she said. "I'll protect Hala."

Without waiting for his response, she launched herself at the attacker, clashing with him in a burst of sparks and fury.

Satora, having just finished off her opponent, joined her in the fight. Now united in purpose, the two women fought in perfect sync—pushing back and eventually defeating the Mutant who had nearly harmed the child.

Meanwhile, Tadanaka refocused, pushing himself harder than before. With a powerful release of wind-infused Reiki, he cut down two more attackers, not holding anything back this time. His movements were heavier, his strikes more deadly. Realizing the tide had turned, the last remaining Mutant turned and ran—escaping into the forest before anyone could chase him.

Tadanaka stepped forward, wanting to pursue, but he stopped himself. With Hala and Yasaze still nearby, the risk wasn't worth it.

CHAPTER SEVEN
A Mission For Redemption

After the intense battle, the group returned to the Gochuu base under heavy silence. No one spoke during the walk back—there was no laughter, no questions, and no relief, only the quiet weight of what had just happened. Once inside, Tadanaka personally carried Hala to his room and gently laid her down to rest. Her small frame curled into the blanket without protest, her eyes already half closed. With the exhaustion from the attack taking a toll on her young body, sleep overtook her quickly.

Tadanaka stood at her bedside for several moments, watching her quietly as she drifted off. When he was certain she was asleep, he stepped out of the room and called the Gochuu Members to him. Suru, Miji, and Satora stood at attention without hesitation.

"None of you are to sleep tonight," Tadanaka said, his voice sharp and commanding. "We protect Hala until morning. She doesn't leave your sight. I'll take her back to the main castle as soon as the sun rises, but until then, nothing—absolutely nothing—gets through us."

The Gochuu Members nodded in full understanding, none of them questioning the order.

Turning away, Tadanaka walked down the hall toward one of the side rooms. His steps were heavy, his expression unreadable. As he reached the door he turned to Kume, who had been silent since they returned.

"Come with me," he said simply.

She followed without a word.

Once inside, he shut the door behind them. The air between them was thick with tension, and the silence dragged for a moment. Then, without warning, Tadanaka stepped forward, unsheathed his blade, and pointed it directly at Kume's chest.

His voice erupted with anger.

"Who were those Mutants?" he demanded. "Why were they ready to kill all of us—but spare you?"

His hand shook slightly from the force of his rage. "You put my niece in danger!"

The accusation hung in the air like a blade over her throat. Kume didn't flinch—but her shoulders slowly lowered, and the fight drained from her face. Knowing she had no ground to stand on, she didn't try to defend herself or talk her way out. Not after what had just happened.

"You want answers?" she said quietly. "Then I'll tell you everything."

Tadanaka didn't lower his weapon, but gave her the space to speak.

Kume took a deep breath, steadying herself. "My sister and I...we've been working with a Mutahawl. We've been planning something for a long time. Our goal was simple—we wanted to kill Master Yuuta."

Tadanaka's eyes narrowed. His grip tightened, but he didn't interrupt.

"We've been hiding, planning, training," Kume continued. "The attacks, the movements, everything was coordinated. It wasn't just me. It was my sister, and ...Gerad."

The name stopped him cold.

Tadanaka's expression shifted. The blade wavered momentarily, then lowered slightly as the name echoed in his mind.

"Gerad?" he repeated slowly. "Gerad of the Torima?"

Kume nodded.

Tadanaka stepped back, the weight of the revelation settling over him. He had heard the name before—everyone had. Among the Mutahawls, there was a known hierarchy.

At the very top were the Obake, the five most powerful and feared Mutants in existence. But just below them stood the Torima—seven deadly Mutants who had slaughtered countless humans and absorbed their Reiki to climb in strength and reputation.

Gerad was the Seventh Member of the Torima. Though he was at the bottom of their ranking, it didn't make him weak. Anyone who reached that level had already surpassed most warriors in the land of Alard. He wasn't just strong—he was dangerous, cunning, and entirely loyal to the cause of reviving the Mutotsu.

"You were working with him..." Tadanaka said slowly, trying to process the weight of the truth. "All this time...you kept this from us."

Kume lowered her gaze. "I didn't know how to tell you. I didn't know if I could even be trusted anymore. But after today...after what happened out there—I couldn't keep it in."

Tadanaka sheathed his blade with a sharp movement and turned away, his hand covering his mouth as he tried to steady his thoughts.

"This is something Master Yuuta must hear," he finally said. "You shouldn't have kept it a secret. Not when it involves a Torima...and especially not when the target is my father."

As the first light of morning crept over the land, Tadanaka, Kume, and Hala prepared to leave the Gochuu base. The atmosphere was quiet, but the tension from the day before lingered in every step they took.

Having agreed to accompany them partway, Yasaze walked with them down the main path until they reached the fork that led toward the castle. There, he offered a brief farewell, stating that he had something to take care of in town and would return later.

Tadanaka nodded, gave him a few final words of caution, and continued with Kume and Hala. As they reached the gates of the main castle, two Toukan warriors were already stationed at the entrance. Without hesitation, Tadanaka turned to them and carefully handed over the young girl. His voice was calm but firm as he gave instructions.

"Take her back home safely. Don't let her out of your sight—not for a second. She's been through enough."

The warriors bowed respectfully, assuring him they would see her home without incident. Tadanaka stood still as they disappeared into the distance with Hala, watching until they were no longer visible. Only then did he turn toward the doors of the castle.

He and Kume entered side by side, their footsteps echoing faintly against the floors. Before they had made it far, they were stopped by a familiar presence.

Shita stood ahead of them in the corridor, her posture composed, her expression cold as always. She regarded the two of them with cool, steady eyes before speaking.

"Tadanaka," she said plainly. "Why have you brought her here?"

While there was no hostility in her tone, the weight behind the question was clear. Shita didn't tolerate games, and she didn't like surprises.

Tadanaka met her gaze without flinching. "Kume has something important to say," he replied. "Information that Master Yuuta needs to hear for himself."

Shita studied them for a long moment, her silence stretching just long enough to make Kume uneasy. Then, without another word, she turned on her heel and began walking down the corridor.

"Follow me," she said.

Neither of them questioned it.

They walked behind her through the hallways of the castle, past guards and servants, until they reached the doors that led to Yuuta Toukan's private chamber. Shita stopped in front of them, glanced back once at Tadanaka and Kume, then stepped aside.

"This better be worth it," she said under her breath.

As Yasaze made his way through the quiet streets of town, the morning trade was just beginning to pick up. Vendors opened their stalls, the scent of fresh bread and herbs drifted from nearby shops, and townsfolk moved about their routines with calm familiarity.

While passing through one of the narrower paths near the bookstore he had visited the day before, his eyes caught a familiar figure among the crowd. Just ahead, walking at a steady pace with book in hand, was Shiro.

A faint smile touched his face as he raised his voice slightly. "Shiro!"

She turned towards the sound of her name, her face brightening with recognition as she saw him approaching.

After exchanging a brief greeting, the two began walking side by side without much discussion. They wandered through the town slowly, their conversation picking up easily as if they had already known each other longer than a day.

Back at the main castle, the doors of the chamber slid opened slowly as Shita, Tadanaka, and Kume entered the hall where Yuuta Toukan awaited them. The ruler of Alard stood before them, his presence as calm and commanding as ever. The atmosphere in the room was still and quiet, yet carried a gravity that could be felt with each step.

Shita and Tadanaka without hesitation, both moved to the center of the room, kneeling before Yuuta in a gesture of deep respect. Kume hesitated for a moment, uncertain, but Shita turned her head slightly toward her. With a single, cold glance from her one visible eye, Shita made her expectations clear. Catching the message without a word, Kume followed their lead, lowering herself onto one knee.

Yuuta's gaze swept over them slowly, his voice calm but firm. "Shita, rise. Stand by my side."

Shita did as commanded and stepped to his right, her posture straight and her expression sharp as always. Yuuta then turned his eyes toward Kume, his tone less severe as he offered a measured greeting.

"You are welcome in this castle, Kume."

Shita's tone was less warm. Her voice cut through the air with quiet authority. "Then tell us," she said, her eye fixed on Kume, "what brings you here to speak with Master Yuuta?"

Tadanaka shifted slightly and took a step forward, explaining everything he had learned from Kume the previous night. He recounted the truth she had confessed—the alliance with a Mutant, the goal of assassinating Yuuta, and the fact that she and her sister had been following the orders of Gerad, one of the seven Members of the Torima.

Shita's voice came low and direct. "You've been working for the Torima?"

Kume didn't answer right away. Her silence filled the chamber, tension creeping into the air.

Tadanaka opened his mouth, clearly about to speak in her defense, but Shita raised her hand without turning.

"I wasn't asking you," she said coldly, her gaze never leaving Kume. "I asked her. Stay silent and let her answer."

Tadanaka, though visibly tense, lowered his head and held his tongue in compliance.

After a moment of hesitation, Kume finally spoke, her voice quiet but clear.

"Yes...I used to."

Shita's expression didn't change. "Then why should we trust a traitor's word?

"Why believe anything you say now?"

Kume looked up, her voice steadier now. "Because I want the truth."

Yuuta tilted his head slightly, studying her with quiet intensity.

"I need to know whether Gerad manipulated me...and my sister," Kume continued. "I don't know what to believe anymore."

Tadanaka spoke up again, this time without interruption, explaining how they were attacked in town by a group of Mutants, and how Kume had risked her life to protect Hala, placing herself between a clawed strike and the child.

For a moment, no one said anything. Then Yuuta stepped forward, his voice as firm as stone but with a trace of something beneath it—respect, or perhaps understanding.

"Fine," he said. "Then find the truth for yourself. And if you do—if you learn that he truly betrayed you—show him no mercy."

Kume lowered her head again, her voice stronger this time. "Understood."

With the tension in the room beginning to shift, Yuuta turned his attention to Tadanaka.

"You lead Kume and the Gochuu," he said. "Track Gerad down and eliminate him. End the threat he poses before more lives are lost."

Tadanaka lowered himself to one knee once more, bowing his head deeply. "We won't fail you, Father."

After receiving their orders from Yuuta, Tadanaka and Kume stepped out of the audience chamber, passing beneath the wooden beams and sliding doors marking the entrance. The quiet corridor was lit by the soft glow of morning filtering in through narrow slats in the walls.

Neither of them spoke as they moved through the castle grounds, their sandals brushing against the smooth pathway leading out into the courtyard.

Back inside, Shita remained beside Yuuta, her arms loosely folded within her sleeves. She stood motionless for a moment before speaking.

"Are you sure they can handle this?" she asked, her voice low but steady. "Gerad isn't just another rogue Mutahawl."

Yuuta didn't look at her directly. His gaze remained fixed ahead, calm and unreadable. "They'll be fine," he replied. "Tadanaka's judgment is sound, and Kume has a reason to fight. If she's truly changed, we'll know soon enough."

Shita gave a small nod, turned, and quietly exited the chamber.

Outside, just as Tadanaka and Kume stepped onto the walkway leading toward the main gate, they heard familiar footsteps approaching from behind. Shita caught up to them, her pace unhurried and her presence as composed as ever. She stopped a step behind them, offering a brief parting remark.

"Good luck with your mission," she said, glancing toward Tadanaka before her gaze shifted sharply to Kume.

Her tone turned colder, her words precise and unwavering.

"But let me be very clear. If I find out you're lying—if this was all an act—I'll cut down you, your sister, and Gerad...and bury you all together without hesitation."

Without waiting for a response, she turned and walked back toward the castle, her expression unchanged and her steps silent against the stone.

Kume stood still, her jaw tight. Tadanaka looked over at her but said nothing.

By the lake near the Toukan main castle, a soft breeze rippled the water as Yasaze and Shiro sat quietly on the grass. Their shoes were off, toes brushing the cool ground; the sounds of the village felt far away. Here, away from duties and titles, they spoke freely, their words carried gently by the wind.

Their conversation drifting from casual thoughts to more personal questions, Yasaze turned toward Shiro and asked, "Have you ever done any kind of training to develop your Reiki?"

Shiro laughed lightly at the question, the sound soft and genuine. "Not at all. I've never really been drawn to that kind of life. Violence, power struggles...all of it just seems exhausting. I try to look at life from a different angle—one that doesn't always lead to conflict."

She paused briefly before continuing, "What about you? Do you train often?"

The moment the question settled between them, Shiro noticed a shift in Yasaze's expression. He slouched slightly and lowered his gaze, staring at the rippling surface of the lake as if the answer was buried somewhere beneath it.

She leaned in a little, sensing the weight in his silence. "Did I say something wrong?" she asked gently.

Yasaze didn't respond right away. When he did speak, his voice was quiet and almost reluctant. "My name is Yasaze Toukan."

Shiro's eyes widened slightly. "Toukan? You're part of the Toukan family?"

He nodded slowly. "Yes...I'm Yuuta Toukan's youngest son."

There was a long pause before he continued, and when he did, his words came with the quiet ache of someone who had carried the truth for too long.

"But I'm not like my father. Or my brothers. I was born without Reiki. No matter how hard I train, no matter how much I want it, I'll never be strong like them. I'll never be able to stand beside them as an equal. To them, I've always been the one thing a Toukan should never be...powerless."

Shiro remained quiet for a moment, watching him as he stared at the lake, his voice now trailing off into a space somewhere between frustration and resignation.

Then, slowly smiling, she nudged his shoulder lightly. "You know...I think that's kind of awesome."

Yasaze turned to her, confused.

She continued, "You've probably heard this before, but I mean it. You don't feel like a warrior to me, and I don't mean that in a bad way. Fighting wouldn't fit you. You don't carry that same kind of weight— they fight because they have to, but you...I don't know...you seem like someone who wants to understand things before destroying them."

She leaned back on her hands, eyes on the sky now. "Besides, not having Reiki doesn't make you weak. It just means you'll have to find your own strength somewhere else."

Yasaze stared at her for a long moment, unsure of what to say. For the first time in a while, her words didn't make him feel like less.

They made him feel seen.

CHAPTER EIGHT
Sisters On Opposite Sides

Back at the Gochuu base, Tadanaka gathered the Members in the training field, his expression focused and serious as he stood before them. The atmosphere was quiet, each of them sensing the weight of what was about to be said. With everyone present, Tadanaka began explaining the mission assigned to them, detailing every piece of information given to him by his father and Shita. In a clear, steady, and unwavering tone, he emphasized just how critical this mission would be.

"This isn't just another assignment," he said, his eyes scanning each of their faces. "We're being trusted with something that could impact the entire balance of the land. There can be no hesitation, no missteps. This is our moment to rise as the Gochuu—not just to carry out orders, but to show exactly what we're capable of when it counts the most."

It was already late by the time the Gochuu arrived in the outskirts of the Toukan region, moving through the forest with sharp awareness. The dense trees made visibility difficult in the cool air, but Kume led the way with confidence, navigating through narrow, overgrown paths without hesitation. She had been here before—many times—and it showed.

Eventually, they reached the edge of a clearing where a worn-down structure stood in silence. The abandoned temple was large, with several of its outer panels now collapsed and its surrounding stone lanterns cracked and chipped.

Despite its condition, the building had a presence—quiet, heavy, and unnerving.

Kume stopped a few steps from the entrance and turned to the group. "This is it," she said. "Gerad operates from inside. If he's not here himself, his subordinates will be."

Tadanaka studied the building for a moment before giving his orders. He looked to Miji and Satora.

"You two stay out here. Keep your eyes on the perimeter. If anything seems off, don't engage unless I signal for it. I want no surprises."

They nodded, taking their positions without question, and Tadanaka gave them a quick nod. It was time to move.

Tadanaka, Kume, and Suru stepped into the temple fully alert, but found it empty. The silence was brief. A woman emerged from the far side, stepping out of the shadows with a group of Mutants flanking her, their presence quiet but threatening.

Tadanaka took a step forward, hand near his weapon. "Who are you?" he asked firmly.

Kume's voice dropped, filled with unease. "It's my sister...Kuna."

Kuna's eyes passed over Kume without pause, settling directly on Tadanaka. Her expression was cold and steady, her tone sharp with intent. "I'm the one who's going to deliver your head to your father."

Kume tried to reason with her, her voice calm but urgent. "Kuna, please, just listen. You've been misled—Gerad, he's been manipulating—"

"Shut your mouth, traitor," Kuna snapped, cutting her off before she could finish. "You turned your back on everything we fought for. You sided with the ones who destroyed our family."

Kume tried again, but Kuna didn't care to hear another word. Lunging forward without hesitation, she attacked her sister mid-sentence. There was no more space for words—only the clash of intent and the bond between them breaking apart.

Before anyone could move, Kume turned slightly toward Tadanaka and Suru while clashing with her sister, her voice firm but calm. "Please...don't interfere. Let me handle her."

Though hesitating for a moment, Tadanaka understood. He gave her a brief nod, then turned his attention to the Mutants beginning to close in. As he stepped forward to meet them alongside Suru, the fight broke out in full.

While Tadanaka and Suru engaged the enemy, steel clashing with claws and Dark Reiki flaring through the air, Kume found herself locked in a brutal exchange with her sister. Kuna showed no hesitation in her attacks.

Her strikes were fast, aggressive, and relentless—driven by pain and betrayal.

Kume, on the other hand, fought defensively. She blocked, dodged, and countered, but never aimed to wound. In her calculated movements, she was careful not to land any fatal blows. Even as she fought, she kept trying to speak over the clash of blades and energy.

"Kuna, please listen to me!" she shouted between strikes. "You're wrong! Gerad's been using us. Everything we believed in—he twisted it!"

But her words didn't reach. Kuna refused to slow down, refused to acknowledge anything her sister said. Eyes clouded with rage, her attacks didn't waver for even a second.

Meanwhile, Tadanaka and Suru had gained the upper hand. Through coordinated strikes and precise use of their Reiki, they overwhelmed the enemy. One by one, the Mutants fell, until the two warriors stood victorious, their breathing heavy but controlled.

Even after the last Mutant dropped, the clash between Kume and Kuna continued. Blow after blow, neither willing to give in. Kume still held back, hoping—desperately—that her sister would finally hear her.

Just as the clash between the sisters reached its peak, a chilling presence filled the temple. Without warning, Gerad emerged from the far side of the chamber with a group of additional Mutants at his back. His appearance brought an immediate shift in the atmosphere, and Kuna, upon seeing him, disengaged from the fight and retreated quickly to his side.

Kume's eyes widened with disbelief as her sister stood beside the very Mutant she had just risked everything to expose.

"I have to say," Gerad said, his voice calm and mocking as his eyes settled on Kume, "I'm hurt that you chose to betray me...after everything we've built."

His smile was wide, with no trace of remorse in his expression. The moment stretched, tense and uncertain, until Tadanaka, recognizing the scale of the threat, called out without hesitation.

"Satora, Miji—now!"

Within a second, the other Gochuu Members arrived, taking their positions beside Tadanaka and Suru, ready for whatever was about to unfold. The room was silent for a moment, the tension unbearable, until Kume stepped forward, her voice shaking with fury and disbelief.

"You lied to us," she shouted, her hands trembling, her face streaked with tears. "You manipulated everything. You made us believe we were fighting for justice, but all this time...you were hiding the truth."

She took another step forward, barely able to contain herself. "Why, Gerad? Why did you do it? Did you kill them?" Her voice cracked as she screamed the final question. "Did you kill my family?!"

Gerad stood calmly, his eyes never leaving Kume as she demanded an answer. For a long moment, he said nothing, letting the tension rise until it was almost unbearable. Then, with a slow, cruel smile, he gave her the truth she had feared.

"Yes," Gerad said, his voice cold and unfeeling. "I killed your family."

As the words hit Kume like a heavy blow to the chest, Gerad's hand moved with deadly precision before she could even react. Dark Reiki flared around his fingers as he slashed his clawed hand straight into Kuna's chest.

Kuna gasped sharply, the force of the strike lifting her off balance. Her eyes widened in horror as the betrayal she had just heard became reality. Blood spilled from the wound and her legs gave out beneath her, dropping her to the ground.

Gerad stood over her without a flicker of remorse, his claws still stained with her blood. He looked down at her, smiling faintly.

"You were never anything more than a pawn," he said coldly, his voice low enough for only those close to hear it.

Then, without the slightest hesitation, he began to laugh—a deep, cruel laugh that echoed against the stone walls of the abandoned temple.

Kume's scream of agony ripped through the temple the moment she saw Kuna fall. Without hesitation, she rushed toward her sister—but she wasn't the only one moving. Tadanaka, seeing the danger, surged forward at the same time, drawing his weapon and charging straight at Gerad before the Mutant could finish what he started.

The clash between Tadanaka and Gerad was immediate and violent, the force of Tadanaka's strike driving Gerad back several paces away from Kuna's fallen body. Only with Gerad forced to defend himself did Kume reach her sister's side and drop to her knees.

"Kuna, I'm here—stay with me!" Kume cried, pulling her sister into her arms.

Blood was already soaking through Kuna's clothes, the warm, terrible weight of it sinking into Kume's hands. Her heart raced, but she tried to stay calm, brushing the hair from Kuna's face and pressing her hands against the wound.

Across the temple, the Gochuu Members engaged the newly arrived Mutants, each locking into fierce, desperate battles. With two enemies for every Gochuu warrior, the Mutants fought with wild strength, Dark Reiki twisting the air around them.

Tadanaka clashed hard with Gerad, but the Mutant's power was monstrous.

Every exchange between them shook the stone beneath their feet. Even as Tadanaka pushed himself, it was clear that brute force alone wouldn't be enough.

Seeing the odds stacking up against them, Tadanaka made a quick decision. With a sharp breath, he summoned the full strength of his Reiki, letting it explode outward from him. The sudden surge of energy slammed into the surrounding Mutants, forcing them back and giving the Gochuu Members a moment to regain their footing.

Meanwhile, Kume cradled Kuna in her arms, trying desperately to hold onto her. "Don't speak," she whispered through tears. "Save your strength. We'll get you help—you're going to be fine."

But Kuna's breathing was already shallow, her strength fading fast. As her weak and trembling hand found Kume's, she spoke with what little energy she had left.

"I'm sorry...I was wrong..." Kuna whispered. "Please...forgive me..."

Kume shook her head, sobbing harder as she held her sister closer. "There's nothing to forgive. Please, don't leave me. Stay, Kuna. Stay..."

But the life in Kuna's eyes dimmed, her grip loosened, and with a soft, final breath, her hand fell away.

For a long moment, Kume didn't move, the world around her blurring into distant noise. Then, as the truth sank into her chest like a blade, another scream tore from her throat—louder, rawer, filled with a pain no words could carry.

She clutched Kuna's body tightly, sobbing uncontrollably even as the battle raged around her. Nothing else mattered. In that moment, everything else faded away.

Tadanaka fought with everything he had, clashing with Gerad in a battle that pushed him beyond his limits. Blow after blow, he refused to fall, his Reiki clashing violently with the overwhelming power of his opponent. Gerad was unlike any enemy he had faced before—ruthless, fast, and brutally strong. But Tadanaka didn't back down. Even as blood ran down his arms and his breathing grew heavier, he held his ground and kept pressing forward.

The fight dragged on, brutal and relentless. Yet with each exchange, Tadanaka learned—adapting, countering, pushing harder. Inch by inch, he wore Gerad down, until finally, he gained the upper hand. With one final burst of energy, Tadanaka disarmed him and knocked him to the ground. As Gerad fell to one knee, wounded and weakened, Tadanaka raised his blade, ready to strike the final blow.

But just before it landed, a voice called out—strong, emotional, and impossible to ignore.

"Stop."

Tadanaka froze and turned. Kume was walking toward them, her steps heavy with anger and sorrow. Tears ran down her cheeks, but her eyes burned with purpose. Although her expression was unreadable, her voice was steady.

"I'm going to do it," she said.

Tadanaka held her gaze for a moment, then slowly lowered his weapon and stepped aside. Gerad, still on his knees, looked up at her with a bloodstained face. His tone shifted, his voice pleading.

"Kume...wait. Just listen. Let me explain—"

But Kume didn't want to hear another word. She moved swiftly, without hesitation, and drove her blade straight into his face. The force of the strike ended him instantly. Gerad collapsed to the ground, lifeless.

Around them, the last of the Mutants fell as the Gochuu finished their battles. The temple, once filled with chaos and bloodshed, now fell quiet.

Tadanaka turned back toward Kume, his expression softening as he stepped closer. He looked at her, seeing the weight she carried and the pain that wouldn't leave her eyes.

"I'm sorry about your sister," he said quietly. "She didn't know the truth...but she never gave up on your family. She was strong, Kume. She died a warrior."

Kume didn't speak. She dropped her weapon and collapsed into Tadanaka's arms, her body shaking with sobs as the grief finally overwhelmed her. He held her tightly, saying nothing more. There was nothing else to say.

CHAPTER NINE
And Still She Stood

Just as the dust began to settle and the silence returned to the temple, a slow, mocking clap echoed through the air. The sound was sharp and deliberate, immediately putting everyone on edge.

"Well done. Really, that was quite the performance. Damn...you guys are going to make me cry." a voice called out from behind them.

They all turned at once.

A Mutant stepped forward from the far end of the temple, a twisted grin spread across his face. Several others appeared behind him—lesser Mutants, clearly under his command. Their silent, still way of moving exuded a heavy, unnatural pressure.

The Gochuu Members immediately dropped into a defensive stance, readying themselves for another fight...but before anyone could lunge forward, Tadanaka shouted—his loud, commanding voice cutting through the tension.

"Stop! Don't attack him!"

The others hesitated, momentarily confused, but the look on Tadanaka's face made them listen.

"There's something wrong...I feel it. His Dark Reiki—it's different. It's dangerous. Stronger than Gerad's," Tadanaka said, his voice steady but tense.

The Mutant let out a low laugh, clearly amused. "You're smart, kid. I like that," he said, his casual tone laced with menace. "But don't worry—I'm not here to kill your little crew. They're not worth my time."

Tadanaka kept his eyes locked on the Mutant, his body tense, ready for anything. "Who are you, and what do you want?" he asked cautiously.

The Mutant gave a slow, exaggerated bow. "My name is Seken. Third seat of the Torima. It's nice to meet you, Toukan. So, tell me—do you want to play for a bit?"

SEKEN

The moment the name left Seken's mouth, Tadanaka's expression shifted. His eyes widened in alarm, and his stomach dropped. There was no time to think— only to act.

"Run!" he screamed to his team. "All of you—go!"

Tadanaka launched himself forward with no hesitation, charging at Seken with everything he had, determined to buy his team the time they needed to escape.

Seken moved through the fight with ease, barely making any effort as he handled Tadanaka like a child. No matter how hard Tadanaka tried to land a blow, Seken dodged or blocked it without breaking focus, as if he were barely acknowledging the fight at all. With a single motion, he grabbed Tadanaka and hurled him across the temple floor, sending him crashing into the stone wall with a thud that echoed through the chamber.

Tadanaka staggered as he tried to rise, his body aching and bruised, but Seken didn't give him a moment to breathe. Advancing again, he grabbed Tadanaka by the shoulder and slammed him to the ground once more, his strength completely overwhelming. Then, unable to stand by any longer, the Gochuu Members began to step forward, their expressions filled with concern and fury.

But before they could move, Tadanaka shouted at them with everything he had.

"Stay back! Don't interfere!"

His voice cracked from pain and desperation, stopping the Gochuu in their tracks. Seken turned his head toward them and grinned.

"If any of you take another step," he said, his tone dark and casual, "I'll kill every single one of you where you stand."

The warning wasn't loud, but it carried a chilling weight that froze them in place. Seken returned his attention to Tadanaka, now struggling to his knees, trying to hold on despite the punishment he'd already taken.

"You're a Toukan, aren't you?" Seken said mockingly as he walked over. "I thought you'd be more fun."

With a smirk, he placed his foot on Tadanaka's head and slowly forced him back to the ground, pinning him without resistance. Tadanaka clenched his fists, trying to push up, but his body wouldn't respond—he was too worn down, and Seken's pressure was too strong.

"This is disappointing," Seken muttered, shaking his head. "I expected so much more from someone carrying that name."

Tadanaka could do nothing but lie there, crushed not just by the strength of his enemy, but by the unbearable realization that, right now, he was completely outmatched.

Suddenly, without warning, Miji and Satora sprang into action, launching themselves at Seken with everything they had. Their attacks weren't meant to win—they were a distraction, just enough to force Seken's attention away from Tadanaka for a few precious seconds.

In that brief window, Suru rushed forward, grabbing Tadanaka's battered body and hoisting him over his shoulder without hesitation. The moment Suru secured him, Miji and Satora immediately broke off their assault, retreating quickly without wasting a second.

Kume, tears still staining her cheeks, gathered her sister's lifeless body in her arms and followed the others as they fled from the temple, moving as fast as their wounded and exhausted bodies could carry them.

The Mutants standing beside Seken tensed, ready to give chase, bloodlust clear in their eyes. But before they could move, Seken raised a hand lazily, his sinister smile widening as he watched the group escape into the night.

"Let them go," he said calmly, voice dripping with cruel amusement. "I have a feeling...things are about to get very interesting."

And with that, Seken lowered his hand, watching silently as the wounded Gochuu disappeared into the darkness.

The group was battered and breathless by the time they reached the main castle, clothes torn and stained from the brutal encounter. Without wasting a moment, the attending guards and servants rushed forward, helping them carry Tadanaka and Kuna straight to the Infirmary located within the castle grounds.

The atmosphere inside the Infirmary was heavy and tense. Several doctors and healers immediately surrounded the two injured bodies, trying to assess the damage and stabilize them. The healers worked with quick, practiced movements, but it didn't take long for them to reach a grim conclusion.

One of the senior doctors approached Kume, who stood by the door trembling, arms still slightly bloodied from carrying her sister. He lowered his head slightly, his voice gentle but firm.

"I'm sorry," he said. "It's too late. There's nothing we can do for her."

The words hit Kume harder than any wound she had suffered. She stood frozen, her mind refusing to accept it, as the realization sank deeper into her chest like a heavy stone.

While the other Members stayed by Tadanaka's side, Kume left the Infirmary and made her way through the main castle halls, her mind heavy with everything that had happened. She barely lifted her head as she walked, still carrying the weight of her sister's death and the betrayal that had shattered her world. Just as she approached the central corridor, she found Shita waiting for her, standing in her usual quiet posture.

Without wasting time, Shita spoke. "Did you complete the mission?"

Kume stopped a few paces away, gathering herself before answering. "Yes. Gerad is dead. But we ran into another Member of the Torima—Seken. He was too strong. If we hadn't escaped when we did, none of us would have made it."

Shita's gaze remained unreadable. "And the truth?"

Kume swallowed hard, forcing the words out. "Gerad killed everyone. He wiped out my village...my family. He manipulated my sister and me for his own gain. I should have seen it sooner. I'm sorry for the trouble I caused."

For a moment, Shita said nothing. Then she asked a final question. "Your sister?"

The mention of Kuna brought the sting of fresh grief. Kume lowered her head, unable to hide the tears welling in her eyes. "She's gone," she said in a low voice.

Shita's expression didn't change, but her voice softened slightly. "I see. You don't have to say anything more. You go; I'll deliver the full report to Master Yuuta myself."

Kume managed a quiet "Thank you" and turned to leave, her steps slow.

Before she could get far, Shita called out again. "Where will you go?"

Kume stopped immediately and turned fully to face her, lowering her head slightly out of respect before answering. "I'm going to check on Tadanaka first. After that...I'm not sure where I'll go."

There was a silence between them, but Shita finally stepped closer, her tone more official now. "Stay by Tadanaka's side until he recovers, for I need you to relay a message. By my authority as Second in Command, you, Kume, are now appointed the Fifth Member of the Gochuu."

Kume froze, her eyes widening in disbelief. Staring for a moment, she felt something shift inside her—something that had been broken slowly beginning to heal. She bowed deeply, her voice breaking slightly as she spoke.

"Understood!"

Shita gave a slight nod, then turned without another word and walked away. Kume was left standing alone in the corridor, a new purpose beginning to take root in her heart.

Shita made her way to Master Yuuta's chambers and entered with permission. Standing before him with unwavering composure, she delivered her report, recounting every detail of the mission—the death of Gerad, Kume's loyalty, the loss of her sister, and the sudden appearance of Seken, the Third Member of the Torima.

Yuuta sat in silence as he listened, his expression grave, absorbing every word without so much as a nod. When Shita finished, the room fell into a heavy stillness. The weight of the information lingered between them, and Yuuta remained silent for a long moment, his gaze lowered slightly as though lost in deep and distant thought.

Finally, he drew a quiet breath, the resolve returning to his eyes. His voice was calm but absolute when he spoke, leaving no room for question.

"Send word to Ryoze."

In the quiet shade of the forest, far from the noise and conflict that had taken so much from her, Kume laid her sister to rest beneath a bed of soft earth and moss-covered stone. The grave was simple.

The Members of the Gochuu stood with her, saying nothing at first. They didn't need to. Their presence alone was enough to let her know she wasn't alone. Miji remained quiet with his arms crossed and head lowered. Satora, for once, offered no jokes—just a gentle hand on Kume's shoulder. Suru, as always, stood at a respectful distance, silent and watchful.

Kume stood for a moment longer when it was over, her gaze fixed on the grave as the final breeze passed through the trees. She didn't speak, but the tears on her cheeks said everything.

Eventually, they all turned to head back together. Though none of them said it aloud, they shared the same unspoken thought: It was time to return to the Infirmary—to be by Tadanaka's side and wait for him to regain consciousness. After everything that had happened, none of them intended to leave him alone. Not now.

CHAPTER TEN
His Presence, Her Flames

Back at the Infirmary, Kume sat quietly with the Members of the Gochuu outside Tadanaka's room, each of them refusing to leave their captain's side. The hours dragged, filled with little more than anxious waiting and whispered conversations.

The doors to the Infirmary opened suddenly, and two figures entered—a man and a woman, both carrying an unmistakable presence that instantly drew every eye. The man had long, loose hair, with two distinct blue lines marking the skin on his left eye. Beside him walked a woman with jet-black hair streaked with sharp red highlights, her expression cool and her gaze razor-sharp.

Without a single word, the Gochuu Members immediately dropped to one knee, bowing low in respect. Even Kume, who had never seen these two before, instinctively followed their lead. The energy radiating from the man alone was overwhelming, carrying with it an authority so heavy it was impossible not to bow, even without knowing who he was.

The man stopped before them, his voice calm but commanding as he spoke.

"How is he doing?"

Still bowing, Suru answered without hesitation. "He's badly wounded and has suffered many injuries…but the doctors believe he will survive."

The man gave a single nod. He and the woman stepped past them without another word, entering Tadanaka's room and closing the door behind them.

Kume remained kneeling for a moment longer, then leaned slightly toward the others and whispered, "Who are they?"

Still keeping her voice low, Kume asked again, unable to hide her curiosity. Without lifting his head, Suru answered calmly.

"That was Ryoze Toukan, Master Yuuta's eldest son," he said. "Leader of the Nokuba and Tadanaka's older brother. And the woman with him is Naru Akaryu—Ryoze's wife and the co-leader of the Nokuba. She's also the daughter of the leader of the Akaryu Clan."

Kume slowly turned her head toward Suru, her eyes wide with shock as the names sank in. She had heard stories all her life, stories whispered across every village and town, of Ryoze's unimaginable strength and the Nokuba's legendary reputation. To realize that the man who had just stood before her, the man whose presence alone commanded the air around him, was that Ryoze Toukan—it left her stunned in silence.

RYOZE TOUKAN

NARU AKARYU

Inside the room, Ryoze quietly approached his injured younger brother, his steps slow and careful as if afraid to disturb the fragile peace that hung in the air. He knelt beside the bed and gently placed a hand on Tadanaka's forehead, the touch filled with a mixture of sorrow and affection.

Leaning closer, Ryoze spoke in a soft voice, barely above a whisper. "Tadanaka..."

At the sound of his brother's voice, Tadanaka stirred slightly. His eyes, though heavy and clouded with pain, fluttered open just enough to see him. A faint smile touched Tadanaka's lips as he struggled to speak.

"Big brother..." he murmured weakly before his eyelids fell shut once more, slipping back into much-needed rest.

Ryoze remained at his side, keeping his hand resting lightly on Tadanaka's head. His voice was steady, but filled with quiet emotion as he spoke. "Rest now, little brother. Leave everything else to me."

Ryoze and Naru exited the room in silence, their expressions unchanged but their presence heavier than before. As they stepped into the corridor, they turned to face the Gochuu Members who were still kneeling in respect.

"Who was responsible for this?" Ryoze asked, his tone calm but carrying undeniable weight.

Kume raised her head slightly, her voice steady despite the memory. "Seken...the Third Member of the Torima," she replied.

Ryoze's eyes shifted to her with quiet intensity. "Do you remember where he was?"

"Yes, my Lord," Kume answered respectfully, not hesitating for a moment.

There was a brief pause before Ryoze continued. "What is your name?"

"Kume," she responded, lowering her gaze slightly in reverence.

Ryoze gave her a nod. "Stand up. You're coming with us. You'll be our guide and lead us to where you last saw him. As for the rest of you," he said, turning to the Gochuu Members, "your duty is here now. Stay by Tadanaka's side, and do not leave him—not for a moment—until he recovers."

Without delay, the Gochuu Members bowed lower, their voices in perfect unison. "Understood!"

Ryoze glanced at Naru, then back at Kume. "Let's move. Naru, with me. Kume—you lead."

Without further words, the three of them turned and left the Infirmary together, their footsteps firm as they set out toward the place where

Seken had last been seen, the tension between them silent but heavy with purpose.

When Tadanaka finally opened his eyes, the familiar ceiling of the Gochuu base greeted him. His body still ached from the battle, but he managed to sit up slightly and called out for his team. Within moments, Suru, Miji, and Satora rushed into the room, their faces lighting up with relief as they saw their captain awake and breathing.

"Tadanaka!" Satora said, barely containing her excitement. "We're so glad you're awake!"

Tadanaka gave them a tired but warm smile before quickly asking, "What happened? And where's Kume?"

Suru, stepping forward as the calmest among them, answered respectfully.

"Lord Ryoze and Lord Naru have taken her. She is guiding them to where Seken was last seen."

Hearing that, Tadanaka immediately tried to push himself out of bed, determination flashing in his eyes. "I have to go. I have to support my brother— he shouldn't face this alone."

But before he could stand fully, another voice cut through the room, firm and unmistakable.

"You will do nothing but rest. Leave it to your elder brother."

Tadanaka froze and turned his head toward the doorway, where Master Yuuta entered the room with Shita walking silently beside him. Instantly, all the Gochuu Members dropped to their knees, bowing deeply before their ruler.

Yuuta stepped closer, his expression softening as he looked at his son. "You've done well, Tadanaka. I am proud of you. You fought bravely, and you protected your comrades. If blame lies anywhere, it is with me. I underestimated the Torima's strength. But now, your task is simple. Rest. Trust your brother to handle what comes next."

Tadanaka lowered his head in deep respect, his voice firm but emotional. "Yes, Father."

Deep within the quiet forests bordering the Toukan lands, Ryoze, Naru, and Kume moved swiftly through the dense trees, the path ahead narrow and uneven. Kume led them forward, her heart pounding in her chest with every step. Though she did her best to hide it, the unease gnawed at her.

After a while, Ryoze's voice broke the silence. "Are we on the right path?" he asked, his tone calm but sharp enough to leave no room for guessing.

Kume glanced back briefly, her voice respectful but urgent. "Yes, my Lord...but I beg you to reconsider. We still have time to turn back and request support from Lord Shita. Seken is not like the others. I have never seen anyone wield power like his, and he commands Mutants that are dangerously strong. There are only three of us...if we face him like this, we are surely walking to our deaths."

There was a short pause. Ryoze, walking just behind her, gave a small, almost amused smile. "Is that so?" he said in a tone that made it unclear whether he was taking her concern seriously or simply humoring her.

"Yes, my Lord," Kume pressed, trying to make him understand. "Please reconsider."

Before Ryoze could reply, Naru—who had been walking silently at his side— turned her sharp gaze toward Kume. Her tone, though casual, cut straight through the tension like a blade. "You've got quite the mouth on you, kid," she said, a smirk tugging at the corner of her lips. "But I'll make you a deal, little coward. Lead us to Seken like you promised, and once we find him, you can run back to the castle with your tail between your legs. Leave the real work to us."

Kume's face flushed with a mixture of shame and frustration, but she bowed her head low and replied with discipline, "Yes, Lord. I will obey."

Ryoze said nothing further, only giving a small glance to Naru, who simply shrugged with a half-grin. The three pressed forward in silence, the air growing heavier with every step as they neared their inevitable confrontation.

The three of them finally arrived at the outskirts of a crumbling stone temple deep within the woods—the place where Seken had last been seen. The old structure loomed before them, silent and cold, its presence heavy with the lingering traces of Dark Reiki.

They stopped at the edge of the clearing, and for a moment, only the sound of the wind rustling through the trees filled the air. Naru turned to Kume with a casual glance, her voice carrying that same sharp edge it always had. "Alright, kid. You've led us this far. You can head back now if you're scared. No one will blame you."

Kume stood still, her hands clenched tightly at her sides. The fear was obvious on her face, her heart pounding so loudly she could hear it in her ears. A thousand thoughts raced through her mind—of death, of survival, of the hopeless odds they were about to face. She lowered her head for a brief moment, gathering every ounce of courage she had left.

The fear was still there when she lifted her eyes again, but it was no longer in control. Her voice shook slightly at first, but grew stronger with every word. "I will stay. I will fight with you. If I am fated to die here, then so be it."

There was a moment of silence. Ryoze gave her a small nod of approval, a faint but genuine smile touching his lips. "Well said," he replied, his voice steady and calm.

Naru chuckled quietly, her sharp, red-streaked hair catching the light as she crossed her arms. "The brat turned out to have some guts after all," she said with a smirk, her tone halfway between mocking and impressed.

They stepped cautiously into the temple, the air inside thick with the oppressive weight of Dark Reiki. Standing at the center of the temple, surrounded by a group of looming Mutants, was Seken—his figure relaxed, almost casual, as if he had been expecting them for some time.

The moment Seken laid eyes on them, a wide, unsettling smile spread across his face. "Finally," he said, his voice carrying an edge of mocking amusement. "I was starting to get bored waiting for you."

Kume stiffened at the sound of his voice, her body instinctively tensing. Fear rose sharply inside her, twisting her stomach into knots, though she tried her best to conceal it. Still, the trembling in her fingers and the way she shifted her stance betrayed her more than she realized.

Seken's sharp gaze landed on her, and he tilted his head slightly, his grin widening. "You…I remember you, girl," he said, almost with a sense of amusement. "Please tell me you've brought stronger friends this time." One of the Mutants standing beside him, eager to please their master, let out a low chuckle. "It won't matter who she brings," the Mutant said with a sneer. "It'll all be a waste. Nobody can match Lord Seken."

Kume's breathing grew heavier, each breath shallow and tight as the pressure of Seken's Dark Reiki wrapped itself around the temple. She clenched her fists at her sides, willing herself not to panic.

Noticing her distress, Ryoze spoke calmly, his voice steady enough to cut right through the tension. He didn't even look at Seken yet; instead, he kept his focus solely on Kume. "Calm down, kid," Ryoze said. "Stay focused. Now tell me," he continued, his tone completely even, almost casual, "which one of them hurt my little brother? Which one is Seken?"

Seken laughed loudly, his voice full of mockery as it echoed through the abandoned temple. "Brother? That little Toukan weakling was your brother? He was nothing but a roach beneath my feet," he said, grinning cruelly.

Kume, her hands slightly trembling, pointed toward him. "It's him... he's Seken," she said quietly.

Seken's grin widened as he looked back at Ryoze. "I'll humiliate you just like I humiliated your younger—"

He never finished the sentence.

In a blur of motion so fast it almost didn't register, Ryoze disappeared from where he stood and reappeared right in front of Seken's face. There was no warning, no time to react. Ryoze's hand closed around Seken's head with terrifying force, and without a shred of hesitation, he slammed it straight into the stone floor. The ground cracked beneath the impact, and Seken's body collapsed lifelessly, his skull crushed beyond recognition.

Seken—the Third Member of the Torima—was dead before he even realized the battle had started.

Kume stood frozen in shock, her breath caught in her lungs. She had expected a fight, a struggle, some sort of grand clash between powerful warriors. But this—this was no battle. It was execution.

For a moment, there was only silence. Ryoze stood without a word and began to walk away. Even the Mutants surrounding Seken seemed frozen in place, stunned by how quickly their leader had been killed. But shock turned to rage, and in the next heartbeat, they moved. Four Mutants launched themselves from all directions, their claws gleaming, their bodies surging with Dark Reiki as they rushed toward Ryoze, determined to avenge their fallen master.

The Mutants closed in like a pack of wild beasts, reckless in their fury, convinced that even if one fell, the others would tear Ryoze apart. But Ryoze never even glanced at them. He continued walking forward, calm and unhurried, as if their existence was beneath his concern.

But before their attacks could reach him, the air shifted.

With a sudden burst of speed, Naru moved. A flash of fire streaked through the darkened temple, her blade slicing through the space between them with deadly precision. Her body became a streak of heat and steel as she ran straight through the four Mutants, her movements so fast that their eyes barely had time to follow.

In a single, seamless motion she cut them down, her blade passing cleanly through hearts and skulls. Trails of faint smoke followed in her wake, the Fire Reiki clinging to the air where she had moved.

By the time the Mutants hit the ground, lifeless and silent, Naru had already caught up to Ryoze. Without missing a step, she calmly sheathed her sword and started walking beside him, as if nothing had happened.

Kume remained frozen in place, her body refusing to obey as the shock of everything she had just witnessed sank in. The slaughter had ended almost before it had begun, the enemies who had terrified her cut down without hesitation, without struggle. Her legs gave out and she collapsed onto her knees, hands pressed to the cold, cracked floor of the temple as she stared at the bloodied scene around her, struggling to process what had just taken place.

Ryoze and Naru walked past her without pausing, their steps calm and deliberate, as if the destruction they had left behind was of no concern to them. They moved together, steady and composed, their presence unaffected by the violence still lingering in the air.

As they reached they reached temple entrance, Naru cast a glance over her shoulder, her sharp eyes locking onto Kume.

"Get up, brat—or do you plan to rot here with the rest of them?" Naru said without stopping.

Without waiting for a response, she turned away and continued after Ryoze, her posture relaxed and unbothered, leaving Kume to gather herself alone in the aftermath of the battle.

With trembling hands, Kume slowly pushed herself to her feet, swallowing the lingering fear in her chest as she stumbled forward, forcing her body to move and follow them into the night.

CHAPTER ELEVEN
So We Never Fall Again

The Members anxiously waited for any news at the Gochuu base, their thoughts heavy with worry and questions they didn't dare speak aloud. When Kume finally returned, stepping through the entrance with a worn but steady expression, the tension broke almost instantly. Relief washed over the group, and they quickly gathered around her, glad to see she had made it back safely.

Tadanaka was the first to move, his concern evident as he rushed to meet her. Without wasting a second, he asked her where Ryoze was. Kume caught her breath before answering, explaining that Lord Ryoze had gone ahead to report the results of the mission directly to Master Yuuta.

Still uneasy, Tadanaka pressed further, asking her what had happened. For a moment, Kume struggled to find the words, her mind still replaying the overwhelming scene she had witnessed at the temple. She lowered her head slightly, her voice trembling with awe as she finally spoke.

"What incredible power...Lord Ryoze defeated Seken in a single blow, and Lord Naru cut down all the Mutants in less than a heartbeat. I have never seen anything like it...it was beyond anything I could have imagined," she said, the disbelief still fresh in her voice.

The other Members exchanged shocked glances, clearly trying to process what they had just heard.

All except for Tadanaka.

He smiled, pride unmistakable on his face, and crossed his arms with a nod of certainty. "As expected of my older brother," Tadanaka said proudly. "He was the one who trained me, the one I've always aspired to become. Seken never stood a chance against him."

Without waiting for anyone to respond, Tadanaka turned toward the exit, his resolve burning bright. "I have to go see him," he declared, and without another word, he left the base and made his way to find Ryoze.

Meanwhile, back at the Toukan main castle, Ryoze and Naru made their way into Master Yuuta's chamber. As they stepped inside, they immediately lowered themselves into a respectful bow, their movements sharp and disciplined. Yuuta, seated at the head of the room, offered them a warm but measured welcome, his presence as commanding as ever. With a calm voice, he asked how their mission had gone.

Ryoze was the first to answer. In a steady and direct tone, he reported that the mission had been completed successfully and, more importantly, that no one under their watch had been harmed. Naru gave a slight nod in agreement, standing silently by his side.

Hearing the news, Yuuta allowed a rare smile to cross his face. He praised them both for their swift and decisive handling of the threat, his approval clear in his words and in the proud look he gave his eldest son and his daughter-in-law.

After leaving Yuuta's chamber, Ryoze and Naru made their way down the corridor and soon crossed paths with Shita. She approached them with a small smirk and a knowing look.

"So, since you're both back," Shita said casually, her tone light with amusement, "I'm guessing Seken is dead."

Ryoze chuckled under his breath, a rare edge of frustration hidden in his voice. "I wish I could've taken my time with him," he admitted, his eyes narrowing slightly, "but when I thought about what he did to Tadanaka, my anger got the better of me. I ended it in one blow."

Shita laughed and shrugged.

"Oh well, at least you finished the job," she said without sympathy. "Did you stop by to check on Tadanaka yet?"

Ryoze shook his head and answered honestly, explaining that after reporting to Master Yuuta, he hadn't yet had the chance. As Shita turned to excuse herself and continue on her way, Naru interrupted her, casually inviting her to join them for dinner at their home.

Shita paused for a moment, then accepted the invitation with a brief nod, falling into step beside them.

Before they could get far, a loud voice cut through the air.

"BROTHER!!" Tadanaka called out, sprinting across the courtyard toward them. His robes were still loose from recovery, but his face was lit with pure relief.

He rushed up to Ryoze and immediately bowed low, voice filled with guilt.

"You're back...I wanted to join you, believe me, but Father stopped me. I'm sorry...I'm sorry I got defeated," Tadanaka said shamefully, still bowing deeply.

Without a word, Ryoze reached out and placed a firm but gentle hand on Tadanaka's head. He let out a soft laugh, the kind only an older brother could manage.

"There's no need to apologize," Ryoze said warmly. "I heard you defeated a Member of the Torima. You've gotten stronger, Tadanaka... and you made me proud."

Tadanaka finally lifted his head, his face brightening at his brother's words.

"Now," Ryoze added, motioning toward the path ahead, "come and join us for dinner."

Together, Ryoze, Naru, Shita, and Tadanaka smiled and walked side by side, making their way back toward Ryoze's castle under the settling evening sky.

As they arrived, Hala and Yasaze were already waiting to greet them. The moment Hala spotted them, she let out a cheerful cry and ran forward without hesitation, leaping into Tadanaka's arms with all the excitement of a child who had waited far too long. Tadanaka laughed as he caught her, steadying her easily despite still recovering from his injuries.

Without missing a beat, Hala stretched out her small hands toward Shita, who leaned down and scooped her up with a rare, gentle smile. Hala clung to her happily, clearly having missed her as much as the others.

The evening settled into a warm, comforting rhythm as they all gathered around for dinner. They sat close together, Hala sitting right on Shita's lap throughout the meal, babbling happily while everyone listened with patient smiles.

At one point during the meal, Tadanaka glanced up, his expression growing more serious, and turned his attention toward Shita.

"I heard you made Kume an official Member of the Gochuu," he said respectfully, his voice steady but filled with gratitude. "Thank you, Lord Shita."

Shita, still holding Hala securely against her, looked over at him with a thoughtful expression. She gave a slight nod before replying, her voice quieter now, carrying an unusual warmth beneath her usual sharpness.

"Poor girl..." Shita said, almost to herself. "She had nowhere left to go. After everything she's been through...she at least deserves a place where she can stand on her own two feet again."

The room grew a little quieter after her words, the weight of everything they had all been through hanging in the air. But the comfort of being together again softened the mood, and for a little while longer, they simply enjoyed the peace of the evening.

After dinner, the castle took on a relaxed, almost lively atmosphere. Shita and Yasaze were busy entertaining Hala in the main hall, chasing her around playfully as the little girl's laughter echoed off the walls. Naru moved quietly nearby, gathering the empty plates and setting about cleaning up, her movements graceful and efficient as always.

Ryoze, however, noticed that Tadanaka had quietly slipped away from the noise and was now sitting alone near the edge of the garden, his gaze distant as he stared out into the night. Ryoze quickly made his way over and lowered himself beside his younger brother, resting his arms casually across his knees.

"What's on your mind, Tadanaka?" Ryoze asked in a calm, steady voice, already sensing the weight that was pressing on his brother's shoulders.

Tadanaka hesitated for a moment, his hands clenching slightly before turning to face him. "Brother...may I request something of you?" he asked, his tone respectful but carrying a hint of desperation.

Ryoze offered him a small smile, the kind of smile that only family could share, and without a second thought, replied, "Anything for you, little brother. Speak your heart."

Tadanaka straightened his back, his eyes burning with determination as he said, "Please train me again. I have to get stronger. If I don't, I'll never achieve my dream of joining the Nokuba and serving under your command."

For a moment, Ryoze simply studied him, his sharp gaze detecting the sincerity written across every line of Tadanaka's face. Finally, he placed his hand on Tadanaka's head as he always did, his voice serious but filled with pride.

"Tadanaka...you are already the leader of the Gochuu. They look up to you, trust you, and follow you. You shouldn't want strength just for yourself—you should want it for them, to inspire them to become even stronger alongside you. That's what true leadership means," Ryoze said.

"But if it's training you want, little brother, then you'd better be ready. I won't go easy on you," he continued with a gentle smile.

"Yes, Lord!" Tadanaka said without hesitation, bowing deeply to Ryoze as his heart filled with renewed purpose.

The morning sun rose high over the Gochuu base, casting long shadows across the training grounds where Tadanaka had called his team to assemble. Standing tall before them, his voice firm and steady, he addressed the group with a rare fire in his tone.

"We all saw it with our own eyes," Tadanaka began, sweeping his gaze across each Member, "how easily we were defeated by Seken and his Mutants. No matter how hard we fought, we couldn't stop them. We were powerless...and it almost cost us everything." His fists tightened at his sides, the memory clearly fueling his words. "But starting today, that changes. We will train harder than ever before. The Gochuu will never again know the taste of defeat!"

The Members straightened their backs in response, the shame of their earlier failure burning in their chests. In one voice, strong and determined, they shouted, "UNDERSTOOD!". The words echoed through the grounds, a promise not only to Tadanaka but to themselves.

Without wasting another moment, they threw themselves into training. They sparred fiercely, pushed each other to their limits, and refused to show weakness. Every block, every strike, and every movement carried the weight of their determination to become stronger for the battles ahead.

Tadanaka took his leave as the Members clashed and honed their skills under the growing heat of the day, heading toward Lord Ryoze's side as promised. His heart was focused, his mind already prepared for the brutal training awaiting him.

Meanwhile, Kume stood off to the side for a moment, watching the others with a thoughtful look in her eyes. A new idea had begun to form in her mind—a way she could contribute even more. Without hesitation, she turned on her heel and made her way toward the Toukan main castle, her steps quick and purposeful.

Meanwhile, back in town, Yasaze caught sight of Shiro walking casually through the market. He raised his voice to catch her attention, calling out her name. Shiro turned toward him with a gentle smile, approaching without hesitation.

"Oh, if it isn't Yasaze. What a coincidence," she said lightly. "What brings you out here?"

Yasaze walked up to her, his steps slow, his hands resting behind his back. "A lot has been going on back home," he said with a soft sigh. "I just needed to get away for a bit, clear my head."

Shiro listened patiently, then smiled again and offered to treat him to lunch. Yasaze agreed without much hesitation, appreciating the company. After their meal together, they found themselves wandering through the town, following no particular path, their conversation light and easy. Eventually, their steps took them toward the edge of the woods, where the trees thickened and the crowds thinned.

As they moved closer to the forest, a sudden disturbance caught their attention. A Mutant emerged from the shadows, blocking their way. Instinctively, Yasaze stepped in front of Shiro and ordered her to run, his voice sharp with urgency.

But Shiro stubbornly refused, standing her ground and refusing to abandon him.

The Mutant prepared to strike, but before it could make its move, two Reiki warriors burst from cover, weapons drawn and ready. They overpowered the Mutant in a swift clash, killing it before it could harm either Yasaze or Shiro.

Panting slightly, one of the warriors rushed over to Yasaze and bowed. "Lord Yasaze, are you alright?"

Yasaze gave a brief nod, his voice steady. "Yes Niko. I'm fine. Thank you both."

Shiro, still gripping the edge of her sleeve tightly, turned to him with wide eyes. "Who are they?" she asked.

"They're my bodyguards," Yasaze explained simply. "Assigned by my father to watch over me, though I don't always make it easy for them."

One of the guards stepped forward, his tone bordering on scolding. "Lord Yasaze, please don't run off like that again. If anything were to happen to you, it would be on our heads."

Yasaze smiled sheepishly and gave a small shrug. "I didn't mean to make your job harder. I just needed some time to think."

With the immediate danger subsided, the guards insisted on escorting Yasaze and Shiro back toward the safer areas of town. Shiro politely excused herself once they reached a calmer street, thanking Yasaze for the walk.

Yasaze smiled warmly and dipped his head. "Thank you for the meal," he said sincerely. He turned back toward his guards as she disappeared into the crowd, and they quietly made their way home.

Tadanaka made his way to Ryoze's castle, his steps quick with anticipation.

However, when he arrived, he found that his older brother was not there. He was instead greeted by Naru, who stood calmly at the entrance, arms loosely folded across her chest.

"Lord Ryoze is with Master Yuuta right now," she said, her voice steady. "What brings you here, Tadanaka?"

Tadanaka scratched the back of his head, feeling slightly awkward. "He promised he would help me with my training," he explained, forcing a small smile. "But it's fine. I'll just come back another time."

Naru studied him for a moment, then smiled. "Since you came all this way, it would be a shame to send you back empty-handed," she said. "I'll help you with your training today."

Tadanaka's face immediately lit up with excitement. "Really, Lord Naru?! Thank you!" he said, bowing his head slightly in gratitude.

Naru gave a short laugh, motioning for him to follow. "Come on then. Let's see how much you've improved."

At the main castle, Yuuta, Ryoze, and Shita sat in quiet discussion, their conversation centered around the troubling rise in Mutant activity across Alard. Their tone was serious, each voice carrying the weight of their growing concerns. However, their meeting was interrupted when two of Yasaze's assigned guards hurried into the room, bowing deeply before speaking.

The guards reported that Yasaze and a young woman had been attacked by a Mutant near the outskirts of town. Fortunately, they had intervened in time to prevent any harm. Yuuta's expression tightened as he asked who the woman was. Upon learning her name was Shiro, he nodded approvingly and praised the guards for fulfilling their duty and protecting his son.

With the report finished, Ryoze and Shita excused themselves. Ryoze turned toward the path leading to his own residence, while Shita made her way down the wide, polished walkways of the Toukan Castle. The wooden floors creaked softly beneath her steps, and the open-air hallways gave way to the inner courtyard where her personal quarters were located.

Kume appeared before her, walking with both purpose and clear apprehension in her steps. Coming to a halt in front of Shita, she bowed respectfully. Shita raised an eyebrow slightly, curious at the interruption but saying nothing at first.

"Lord Shita, may I ask you for a favor?" Kume said, her voice steady despite the tension she felt. "You granted me the honor of joining the Gochuu. I wish to live up to your expectations and truly earn my place. Please...I humbly request that you train me."

Shita regarded her silently for a moment, her sharp gaze studying the sincerity in Kume's expression. After a brief pause, she gave a small nod and simply said, "Follow me."

At Ryoze's castle, the sound of training echoed across the yard as Naru faced Tadanaka in a sparring match. Though she had already bested him several times, Tadanaka refused to stay down. Each time he hit the ground, he climbed back to his feet, his breathing heavy but his spirit unbroken. Naru, maintaining her calm composure, advised him to stop rushing blindly and instead focus his Reiki more precisely into his strikes. Her voice was firm but not unkind, guiding rather than discouraging.

As they continued, a familiar presence approached. Ryoze crossed the training grounds with easy steps, observing the two of them with a small smile tugging at the corner of his mouth.

"You're back, big brother!" Tadanaka called out, his face lighting up despite the exhaustion weighing on his body. "Naru has been helping me train while you were away."

"Is that right?" Ryoze replied, glancing over at Naru with a light-hearted tone. "He's gotten stronger, hasn't he?"

Naru gave a small nod, then crossed her arms with a serious look. "He has improved, yes. But he still has a long road ahead of him."

Ryoze chuckled quietly before stepping closer. "Good. Then let's push him a little further. Tadanaka, attack Naru with everything you've got. Focus all your Reiki into one strike."

Tadanaka hesitated for a moment, blinking in disbelief. "Full power? Are you sure, brother?"

Before Ryoze could answer, Naru's sharp voice cut in. "Don't get cocky, brat. Just do as you're told." Her words were blunt, but there was a hint of amusement in her eyes.

Taking a deep breath, Tadanaka gathered his Reiki, feeling the energy surge through his body as he prepared for the attack. Charging forward, he poured every ounce of strength he could muster into a single decisive blow. Naru remained perfectly still, her stance relaxed, almost inviting the attack.

Just as Tadanaka closed the distance between them, Naru's figure flickered and disappeared from his sight. A faint wave of heat brushed past him, a whisper of her Fire Reiki in the air. In the same instant, she reappeared at his back with silent precision. Before he could even turn, a strike landed cleanly between his shoulder blades, knocking him off balance and sending him hard to the ground, the warmth of her energy still lingering as he lay there defeated.

Lying there catching his breath, Tadanaka looked up and gave a small laugh. "As expected...you're really strong, Lord Naru."

"You'll progress in time, little brother," Ryoze said, stepping forward as Naru sheathed her blade and brushed her hands together.

"I'll go check on Hala. I'll leave him in your hands," Naru said lightly, giving Ryoze a nod before turning to leave.

With that, Ryoze took over the training session, his presence both reassuring and challenging, as he prepared to sharpen Tadanaka's strength even further.

Back at the main castle's training field, the wind carried the sharp tension of a test about to begin. Shita stood calmly, arms folded across her chest, eyeing Kume with a level gaze that gave nothing away.

"Come at me," Shita said firmly. "Don't hold back. Attack me as if I were your enemy. But don't expect me to go easy on you."

Kume bowed her head respectfully, her body already tightening with focus. "Understood, Lord Shita," she replied with conviction. Without wasting another moment, she unleashed her full Reiki, the pressure around her intensifying, and charged forward.

Kume moved quickly, her sword flashing as she closed the distance. But before she could even complete her first strike, Shita made a simple motion with her hand. A wave of ice suddenly burst from the ground, snaring Kume's legs and locking them in place. Kume barely had time to react before she lost her balance and fell, landing hard on her back with a dull thud.

Grinding her teeth, she quickly shattered the ice around her legs with a surge of Reiki and forced herself upright. Without hesitation, she lunged again, swinging with more urgency. Shita barely moved her feet; she simply weaved and sidestepped every blow, her movements smooth and effortless.

Kume tried to adjust her speed and find an opening, but before she could shift her strategy, Shita released her own Reiki. The atmosphere around the field shifted instantly, becoming dense and crushing. The pressure dropped like a heavy curtain over Kume's shoulders, pinning her down before she realized what had happened. She collapsed to one knee, gasping for air, the same paralyzing sensation she had felt once before at the Gochuu training field.

Struggling to breathe, Kume clutched at her chest. "Please...Lord Shita...", she choked out between labored breaths, "...please stop...."

Shita remained unmoved, her voice cool but firm. "Endure it. Push through. Find your breath."

Kume gritted her teeth and tried, forcing herself to stay conscious under the immense pressure, but her body trembled uncontrollably. No matter how much she fought it, her lungs screamed for air. Her limbs weakened, and at last, her strength gave out. She collapsed fully to the ground, surrendering to the overwhelming weight.

Only then did Shita release her Reiki, the suffocating pressure lifting as swiftly as it had fallen. Kume lay there, gasping and exhausted, her body heavy with defeat—but her spirit burning with determination to stand again.

CHAPTER TWELVE
The Story She Never Told

Shita and Kume took a break after the intense training session, sitting together along the edge of the field as the cool breeze washed over them. Kume wiped the sweat from her forehead, something catching her eye as she glanced at Shita. Her gaze drifted to the handwrap covering Shita's left hand. Simple but worn, it carried the look of something old yet cherished.

"You know," Kume said, her voice breaking the silence, "Lord Ryoze wears the same exact handwrap on his right hand."

Shita looked down at her hand, giving a small, almost nostalgic smile. "Yeah. I gave it to him when we were little," she said. "Long story."

Kume smiled too, but quickly grew thoughtful. After a moment, Shita leaned back against the wooden beam behind her and asked, "So, what made you want to get stronger?"

Kume's expression turned serious. She clasped her hands together, looking down at them as she spoke. "When we fought Seken...it was like living through a nightmare. No matter how hard we tried, we couldn't even scratch him. But when Lord Ryoze fought him..." Her voice softened in awe. "It was over in an instant. It was like he wasn't even trying. That's when I realized...I needed to become much stronger if I ever want to protect anything in this land."

She paused, gathering her thoughts before adding with a small laugh, "Honestly, Lord Ryoze's strength was scary. He kind of reminded me of you."

Shita chuckled, the rare, easy sound softening the usual sharpness of her presence. "Of course he's strong," she said, her voice light but filled with pride. "We grew up together. We learned to fight side by side, trained every single day, pushing each other past our limits. There was no way he wouldn't turn out strong." She paused before added casually, "Besides, only six people alive today have awakened their Reiki—he's one of them."

Kume blinked, stunned by the casualness of the statement. "Wait... what?!" she asked, struggling to process what she had just heard.

Shita nodded. "That's right. Myself, Lord Ryoze, and Master Yuuta. The other three are the current leaders of the Royal clans—Laitonn, Akaryu, and Abahare."

Kume could barely hide the shock on her face. To think that Lord Ryoze and Lord Shita stood among the only awakened beings in all of Alard—it felt overwhelming, like the gap between her and them had suddenly grown even wider.

Kume hesitated for a moment, then said quietly, "May I ask you something, Lord Shita?"

Shita gave a small nod, her expression calm. "Go ahead."

Gathering her courage, Kume continued, "Your Reiki power is ice… but from what I know, the Toukan family's Reiki has always been wind. How is that possible?"

The question hung in the air. For a brief moment, something in Shita's face shifted—the warmth faded, replaced by a distant, unreadable look. She didn't answer right away.

Seeing the change, Kume quickly lowered her head. "Forgive me, Lord Shita. I shouldn't have asked. Please forget it."

Shita leaned back slightly, her tone shifting into something more like that of a teacher recounting old, buried history.

"There are four major family bloodlines that hold power across the land," she began. "The Akaryu Clan, the Abahare Clan, the Laitonn Clan, and finally, the Toukan Clan, which now rules over all of Alard."

Kume nodded in understanding. "Yes, my Lord. I've heard of these clans," she said respectfully.

A faint, almost nostalgic smile crossed Shita's face before she continued. "But it wasn't always like this. There were always five Royal bloodlines, not four. There was once a fifth clan, known as the Fozuru Clan." She paused for a moment, as if weighing the memories. "The Toukan family had long sought to unite the land under one rule to bring an end to centuries of conflict. And after much struggle, they succeeded. Most of the Royal clans accepted their leadership and worked together to build the peace we have now—"

Her voice hardened slightly. "—all except for the Fozuru Clan."

She continued. "The Fozuru Clan were always hostile to the idea that the Toukan family ruled over Alard," Shita continued, her voice even but carrying the weight of old wounds. "But they never openly opposed the Toukan Clan; for generations, they honored the peace and worked alongside the other Royal clans. But everything changed when Saki Fozuru rose to power."

She paused for a brief moment, letting Kume absorb the shift in tone.

"Over thirty years ago, Saki led the Fozuru Clan down a different path. Unlike his predecessors, he opposed the Toukan family and made it clear he had ambitions of his own. He wanted to rule the land—not as an ally, but as its sovereign."

Kume listened closely as Shita's expression grew a little sharper.

"Lord Asaru Toukan, Master Yuuta's father, was the head of the Toukan Clan at the time. He did everything in his power to keep the peace—sending envoys, offering negotiations, even proposing alliances. But all his efforts were thrown aside. Stubborn and blinded by his hunger for power, Saki Fozuru made his intentions clear. He would see the Toukan Clan overthrown, no matter the cost."

Shita's voice lowered slightly, carrying a heavier tone as she continued.

"After countless efforts to find a peaceful resolution, Lord Asaru realized there was no other choice. The Fozuru Clan could no longer be reasoned with. Their ambition was a threat not just to the Toukan family, but to the peace of all Alard."

She glanced at Kume to make sure she was following before continuing.

"Lord Asaru spoke privately with Master Yuuta, who at that time was still young but already a formidable force. He explained that the Fozuru Clan had to be dealt with, before their rebellion grew into something unstoppable. No matter how painful the decision, it had to be done to protect the land."

Kume leaned in slightly as Shita went on.

"Lord Asaru entrusted Master Yuuta with a grave mission—to gather the finest Reiki warriors from every Royal family, of unmatched strength and loyalty, and lead a final assault against the Fozuru Clan. Back then, Master Yuuta was the leader of the Nokuba, the most elite force in the land. Without hesitation, he called upon his Members, and together with the best Reiki warriors Alard had to offer, he led the attack that would decide the fate of the Fozuru bloodline."

"The Fozuru Clan fought back with everything they had," she continued. "They were fierce warriors, proud and determined to defend their name. But it wasn't enough. Master Yuuta and the warriors he led were too strong. Each fighter had been handpicked for their skill, their power, their loyalty to the peace Lord Asaru had built. They didn't falter; they didn't hesitate. They carried out their mission without mercy."

Kume listened quietly, feeling the weight of the story settle in her chest as Shita's tone grew more solemn.

"The order given to Master Yuuta was absolute: Slay every last Member of the Fozuru Clan. It was not a battle—it was a massacre. Blood stained the ground that day, with the screams of the fallen echoing through the hills. Countless lives were lost, all because one man's ambition clouded his wisdom."

Shita let out a slow breath before continuing.

"In the end, it was Master Yuuta himself who faced Saki Fozuru, the head of the clan. Their battle was fierce, brutal, and short-lived. Saki fought with everything he had, but against Master Yuuta, the strongest Reiki warrior alive, there was never truly a chance. The fight ended swiftly, and with Saki's death, the Fozuru Clan was wiped from existence."

A heavy silence fell between them. Kume sat frozen for a moment, letting the weight of the revelation sink in before finally finding her voice.

"I've never heard of this before," she said quietly, struggling to process everything she had just learned.

"You wouldn't have," Shita replied. "It is forbidden to speak of the Fozuru Clan. Their very existence was erased from history by decree. Only a few still remember the truth."

Kume swallowed, then hesitated before asking the question that burned on her tongue.

"Then...why are you telling me this, Lord Shita?"

For a long moment, Shita didn't answer. Her gaze lowered, the strength in her posture momentarily giving way to something deeper, something painful.

"Saki Fozuru...was my father."

Kume's heart dropped. Her mouth opened slightly, but no words came out. She stared at Shita, stunned, the truth unraveling in front of her faster than she could catch up. She didn't know what to say. She didn't even know if there were words for something like this.

"When Master Yuuta defeated Saki Fozuru, he found me—just an infant, lying alone in the Fozuru main castle. Many of the warriors who stood with him that day urged him to leave me behind, to dispose of me before I could grow into a threat. But Master Yuuta ignored them all. Without hesitation, he picked me up and took me back with him."

She paused briefly, but her tone remained even as she pressed on.

"Bringing me to the castle wasn't well received. Everyone there rejected me. Even Lord Asaru himself—Master Yuuta's father—tried to persuade him to cast me out. They feared I would one day bring misfortune upon the Toukan family...or worse, seek revenge for the blood spilled that day."

Her hand clenched against her leg, though her expression stayed composed.

"But Master Yuuta stood firm. He told them all that he would raise me under his own watch, and if the day ever came when I turned against them...he alone would take responsibility and stop me."

"Master Yuuta brought me back to his castle, and it was there that I first met Lady Tala. She was Master Yuuta's wife—the woman everyone admired—and yet she welcomed me without hesitation. She cared for me, raised me, and loved me as if I were her own daughter. I owe every kindness I have known to her. A year after I arrived, tragedy struck: Lord Asaru passed away, taken by a sudden illness that no healer could cure. With his passing, Master Yuuta ascended to lead the Toukan Clan and with it, the entire land of Alard. That same year, Lady Tala gave birth to Lord Ryoze."

"When I turned seven, Master Yuuta began training Ryoze and me together. Most of our days were spent side by side—sparring, learning, and getting into more trouble than we should've. People in the town didn't make things easy for me. They didn't forget where I came from, and many weren't shy about showing it. I was picked on constantly."

She paused, her smile growing fonder.

"Ryoze always stood up for me. It didn't matter who it was—he would come charging in without hesitation and beat them into the ground. Afterward, Mother would scold us both for getting into trouble, lecturing us like we were criminals, while Master Yuuta would sit there, struggling to hold back his laughter, until Mother noticed and yelled at him too."

Shita let out a quiet, genuine laugh, and for a moment, so did Kume.

"My mother had a precious vase, a beautiful heirloom passed down through generations of her family. I would sometimes sneak into the room just to admire it from a distance. One afternoon, unable to resist, I crept in alone. As I gently touched the vase, admiring its smooth surface, I heard footsteps and voices approaching. Fear gripped me. I panicked, lost my balance, and the vase slipped from my hands, breaking into countless pieces across the floor. My heart dropped. Without thinking, I turned and ran—out of the castle, past the gates, disappearing deep into the woods."

"I hid there for what felt like forever, terrified of what I had done, convinced I had ruined everything. By nightfall, some Reiki warriors found me and brought me back. When they led me into the castle, Mother burst into the room. Her face was filled with anger. I barely managed to say her name before she struck me across the cheek. The sting of it barely registered before she pulled me into her arms, clutching me so tightly I could hardly breathe."

"'Why would you run away?' she sobbed, her voice breaking apart.

"Tears welled in my eyes as I gasped, 'Mom...I broke your vase.'

"She pulled back just enough to cup my face with both hands, her own tears streaming freely.

"'Forget the vase,' she said, her voice trembling. 'I thought I lost you, Shita. I don't care about anything else. Don't ever do that to me again.'

"And right there, in her arms, I broke down, crying harder than I ever had in my life, clinging to the only person who had ever made me feel like I truly belonged."

"By the time I turned ten," Shita continued, her voice steady but carrying a quiet weight, "Lady Tala had already given birth to Tadanaka. Two years later, she gave birth to Yasaze. But when Yasaze was born,

Lady Tala…" Shita paused for a moment, gathering herself. "She died bringing him into this world."

She looked out toward the training field for a moment, as if seeing a memory only she could witness. "The pain of losing her…it was unbearable. I didn't love her like someone who was merely kind to me. No…she was my mother. The only mother I ever knew."

Shita turned back to Kume with a small, almost apologetic smile. "When I turned eighteen, Master Yuuta made both Ryoze and me Members of the Nokuba. He even made me its leader." She laughed softly under her breath. "I remember thinking it was too much for me to handle, but I swore I would be worthy of the trust he placed in me."

She leaned back slightly, her expression growing more thoughtful. "Later that year, during one of our training sessions, my Reiki finally awakened. It was Master Yuuta who witnessed it…and Ryoze too. Afterward, Master Yuuta called me to him and told me the truth— about my real family, about the Fozuru blood that runs in my veins."

There was no anger in her voice, only a calm acceptance. "He thought maybe I would hate him for it. That I would feel betrayed, or torn between two worlds." She shook her head faintly. "But I didn't care about any of that. To me, Master Yuuta and Lady Tala were the ones who raised me. They were the ones who loved me. My blood didn't matter. My past didn't matter. They were my family. They still are."

As Shita finished her story, a faint smile lingered on her lips. Across from her, Kume sat in silent awe, a small smile of her own forming—a bond silently forged between them through the lives they had both lost and the strength they had both found.

Kume shifted slightly, her curiosity getting the better of her. "What about the handwrap?" she asked. "What's the story behind it?"

Shita glanced down at her hand for a moment, a faint, almost nostalgic smile touching her lips. "Ah...the handwrap," she said softly. "This isn't just any cloth. When I was ten years old, my mother—Lady Tala—made it for me herself. She told me it would protect me, that no matter where I went, a piece of her would always be with me." Her fingers lightly brushed the worn fabric, a small, almost unconscious gesture. "I've worn it ever since. Through every battle, every hardship, it's always stayed with me."

Kume listened closely, but another question weighed on her. "If the handwraps were so important to you," she said carefully, "why did you give one of them to Lord Ryoze?"

"After I was appointed leader of the Nokuba, nothing between us really changed," Shita continued, her voice calm. "Ryoze and I still trained together every single day, just like we always had, and we continued to go on missions side by side without fail. It didn't matter how high our titles rose; our bond stayed the same. After some time had passed, Master Yuuta left the castle to meet with the Members of the Haras."

Kume shifted slightly, her curiosity clear. "Members of the Haras? Who are they?" she asked.

"You don't know?" Shita replied, a faint smile crossing her lips. "The Haras are the three leaders of the Royal clans—aside from the Toukan Clan. Each one of them serves directly under Master Yuuta's authority. They have been entrusted with guarding one of the four glass plates that, if reunited, could revive the Mutotsu. The fourth plate, however, remains under the protection of the Toukan family."

Shita let out a slow breath before continuing. "While Master Yuuta left to meet with the Haras, he placed me in charge of the castle's defenses. Everything seemed normal at first, but as I made my rounds, I couldn't shake off this heavy, uneasy feeling. It was like the air itself had turned heavier, thicker. Something was wrong, and deep down, I knew it."

Her expression hardened at the memory.

"I immediately went to check on the glass plate stored within the main hall of the castle," Shita said. "And that's when I saw him— for the first time. Standing there, calmly approaching the plate, was Shen Danbu."

Kume's eyes widened, her voice bursting out before she could stop herself.

"Shen Danbu?! The Mutant leader?!"

"Yes," Shita replied with a grim nod. "I've killed many powerful Mutants in my life, some of them far stronger than ordinary men, but no one...no one has ever carried the kind of Dark Reiki that he did. Not even close."

Her hand tightened slightly around the hilt of her blade as she spoke, as if remembering the weight of the moment.

"He simply stood there, staring at me with a smile, as if he had expected me. He knew Master Yuuta wasn't present. He made his move exactly when he thought no one strong enough could stop him. I didn't waste time thinking—I unleashed my Reiki and charged at him."

"He was incredibly strong," Shita said, her voice dropping low with the weight of memory. "I had never faced an enemy like him before. I gave it everything I had, every ounce of my strength, every bit of my training...but even so, he still overpowered me."

Kume's eyes widened, stunned. "He overpowered you, Lord Shita?!" she asked, barely able to believe it.

Shita gave a small, humorless smile and nodded. "He did. And then... Ryoze arrived. I remember it so clearly. The moment I saw him, my heart nearly stopped. I screamed at him to run, to get away from there as fast as he could. I knew if he stayed, Shen would kill him without a second thought. I was so panicked, so torn between trying to fight and trying to protect him, that I lost focus for just a moment."

Her hand absentmindedly brushed near the eyepatch covering her right eye.

"And that's when it happened," she continued quietly. "Shen took advantage of my distraction. He launched an attack at Ryoze, and without thinking, my body just moved. I threw myself between them. The next thing I knew...his attack struck me full in the face." She tapped the side of her eyepatch lightly. "That's when I lost my right eye."

Kume swallowed, her heart twisting at the thought. "So...you saved Lord Ryoze's life?" she asked gently.

Shita went quiet for a long moment, her gaze distant. Then she smiled, soft and proud. "No," she said simply. "He saved mine."

Kume's brows furrowed in confusion, but she said nothing, sensing there was more.

"After I fell," Shita said, "I begged Ryoze to run. I begged him not to look back. But Ryoze refused. He stayed, standing between me and Shen. I could barely lift my head, but I saw it happen. Right there, in the middle of the battlefield...Ryoze's Reiki suddenly erupted."

Her voice grew softer, almost reverent. "It wasn't just strong—it was overwhelming. Raw, powerful, pure. It happened because he was terrified he would lose me. His emotions forced the awakening. Even Shen felt it...and realized instantly that he couldn't win against the two of us together."

Shita exhaled slowly, the memory still vivid. "Rather than risk his life, Shen Danbu fled. That day, Ryoze awakened his Reiki. That day, he saved both our lives."

Shita's voice softened as she continued, her hand resting lightly over the handwrap she wore.

"After Shen fled, Ryoze ran to me. He was terrified when he saw the blood, when he realized I had lost my eye. He kept apologizing, over and over, blaming himself. But all I could do was smile at him."

A faint, nostalgic smile touched Shita's lips.

"I told him...if it weren't for him, I wouldn't have just lost an eye. I would have lost my life. I thanked him for saving me."

She paused as if reliving the moment, before continuing.

"Then I took off my right handwrap—the one Mother had made for me—and tied it around his hand. It was my way of telling him...we would always be a team. That no matter what happened, we would always have each other's backs."

Shita glanced down at the handwrap on her own hand, her smile lingering with quiet pride. Across from her, Kume sat silently, smiling.

The evening between Shita and Kume slowly came to a close, with a quiet understanding lingering between them—one built on trust, loss, and the will to move forward.

CHAPTER THIRTEEN
The Gathering And The Fall

Time passed, and the world around them kept changing. Under Tadanaka's leadership, the Gochuu pushed themselves harder than ever before. Day after day they trained relentlessly, sharpening their skills and strengthening their bond. Seasons shifted quietly over Alard, and before they realized it, a full year had passed, each of them stronger, wiser, and more determined than the ones they had been.

As Yasaze and Shiro strolled through the town's bustling streets, their conversation was interrupted by the sudden commotion of a boy darting past them clutching a handful of stolen food. The shop owner, red-faced and furious, chased after the boy, shouting for him to stop. Before the situation could escalate further, Yasaze stepped in. Moving calmly between the boy and the enraged merchant, he reached into his robe, pulled out a few coins, and offered them to the owner. The man hesitated for a moment before grudgingly accepting the payment, allowing the boy to slip away without further punishment.

After settling the matter with the shop owner, Yasaze approached the boy, his expression calm but serious. He knelt down to the boy's level, speaking gently.

"Why were you stealing?" he asked.

The boy fidgeted with the hem of his tattered shirt, his eyes darting nervously around. After a moment of hesitation, he finally spoke. "I live in a small village not far from here," he said quietly. "A few months ago, some bandits took over. They expect a payment every month from everyone, or else…"

His voice caught, but he pushed through, determined to explain. "My parents couldn't pay what they asked. They—" He swallowed hard. "They made an example of them. They killed my parents in front of everyone, just to show what would happen if anyone disobeyed."

Yasaze stayed quiet, letting the boy continue at his own pace. The boy's fists clenched tightly as he went on.

"I have a little sister," he said. "She's too small to understand what's happening."

"I stole because…because someone has to take care of her."

Moved by the boy's story, Yasaze asked gently, "Why didn't the villagers report the bandits to the Reiki warriors? Surely someone could have helped."

The boy shook his head, his eyes wide with fear. "The bandits said that if anyone told, they would kill the entire village. Not just the families, but everyone. No one wants to risk it."

Yasaze and Shiro exchanged a glance, both moved by the boy's story. Without a moment's hesitation, Yasaze placed a reassuring hand on the boy's shoulder. "Don't worry. I'll help you. We'll save your village," he said firmly.

The boy's eyes widened in disbelief, his small frame trembling as if he could hardly believe the words he had heard. Yasaze gave him a small smile, then turned to Shiro. "Let's go."

Without wasting any time, Yasaze, Shiro, and the boy made their way toward the Gochuu base. The walk was tense, the boy clutching tightly to Shiro's sleeve as if afraid everything would slip away if he let go. When they arrived, Yasaze immediately sought out Tadanaka, who was overseeing the Gochuu Members' training.

Tadanaka listened carefully as Yasaze explained the situation—the village, the bandits, the threats—and once the story was finished, he didn't hesitate. He called the Gochuu Members together, his voice steady and commanding.

"We leave immediately," Tadanaka said, his eyes burning with determination.

"No innocent village will suffer while we stand by."

Without delay, the Gochuu Members prepared to set out, their faces set with resolve.

The boy led them across narrow paths and winding dirt roads, his small figure moving quickly as if fearing he might lose the way. They finally arrived at the village—a small, worn place tucked between the hills, where the houses were built close together and the air felt heavy with fear. The villagers, wary of strangers, peered out from behind doors and windows as Tadanaka and the others passed through.

They were soon greeted by the village elder, a frail man with tired eyes and a cautious voice. Stepping forward, Tadanaka introduced himself as the leader of the Gochuu. After a long pause, the elder nodded and invited them into a small gathering hall at the center of the village.

Inside, the elder explained the situation in a low, weary tone. He told them that although the bandits were many, only one of them ever came to collect the monthly payments, and that this single collector would arrive tomorrow at dawn. Tadanaka listened closely with his arms crossed, a thoughtful look in his eyes. Once the elder had finished, Tadanaka straightened and answered with quiet determination. "When he comes, I will be the one to deal with him."

Growing pale, the elder immediately shook his head. "You must not interfere," he urged. "If he doesn't return to his group with the money, they will come here themselves—and when they do, they will not leave a single soul alive."

Tadanaka stepped forward, his voice steady but firm, and asked the elder to place his trust in him. He promised that he would not only protect the village, but also get rid of the bandits for good. Though hesitant, the elder finally gave a slow, reluctant nod after seeing the determination in Tadanaka's eyes.

As the sun rose faintly behind the hills the next morning, the villagers hid themselves indoors, peeking through cracks in the walls, their hearts pounding with fear. True to the elder's words, a lone bandit arrived, swaggering into the village with the arrogance of someone who thought he was untouchable. Shouting and cursing, he demanded the payment.

Tadanaka appeared in the open before he could even finish his threats, blocking the center path. Without hesitation, he charged forward and delivered a brutal beating to the bandit, leaving him barely able to stand. Bloodied and gasping, the bandit fell to his knees, pleading for mercy.

"You'll never show your face here again," Tadanaka said coldly.

"I swear! I promise you—I'll never come back to this village!" the bandit cried out desperately.

Tadanaka stepped back and allowed him to flee, watching him stumble out of the village without looking back. But even as he let him go, Tadanaka was not fooled. He knew the man was lying. The bandit would return to his comrades, bringing reinforcements and plotting revenge.

Tadanaka turned to his team, his expression serious. "We follow him," he ordered quietly. "Let's find out where they are and finish this once and for all."

Meanwhile, deep within the misty forests of Alard, Shen Danbu stood atop a cracked stone platform surrounded by an unnatural stillness. Around him, three figures gathered—beings whose very presence warped the air with the weight of their Dark Reiki. These were not ordinary Mutahawls. They were the Obake— the strongest among all the Mutants.

Shen was the First Member of the Obake, the one who had directly inherited a vast share of the Mutotsu's power. To his right stood Lubu, the Second Member, his sheer size and overwhelming energy making him seem like a fortress carved from flesh and bone. Jin, the Third Member, leaned silently against a ruined pillar, his sharp eyes cold and unreadable. Nobu, the Fifth Member, wore a twisted smile on his face, a glimmer of reckless amusement dancing behind his gaze. The Fourth Member, Laya, was missing.

LUBU

JIN

NOBU

Unlike other Mutahawls, the Obake were special. Shen had personally chosen and transformed them, infusing each with a fragment of the Mutotsu's power. This bond made them far more powerful than any other Mutant—beings whose strength rivaled the most formidable Reiki warriors alive.

Shen's gaze swept the clearing, darkening slightly.

"Where is Laya?" he asked, his voice calm yet commanding. "Why didn't she answer my summons?"

Nobu let out a casual chuckle, shrugging without concern. "It's better that she's not here anyway. I can't stand that frozen attitude of hers. And besides, last time we gathered, she almost ended up fighting Jin."

Jin shifted slightly but remained silent, the dark glint in his eye the only acknowledgment of Nobu's words.

Shen gave a dismissive wave of his hand. "Forget it. Let's move on."

Without wasting more time, he explained the reason behind the gathering. Shen spoke of the shifts happening across Alard—the sudden rise in resistance from the Reiki warriors, the disturbing news that two Members of the Torima had already fallen. He told them how the balance was slowly beginning to tip, not in their favor, but against them.

Then Shen spoke the name that had caused the most trouble.

"Ryoze Toukan," Shen said calmly. "Yuuta's eldest son. He is the one who killed Seken."

The name drew an immediate reaction. Nobu's grin widened with interest and he stepped forward slightly, cracking his knuckles in anticipation.

"That Ryoze, huh?" Nobu said. "Thinking he is some kind of tough guy just because he could defeat those weaklings in the Torima. Please, Shen, allow me to handle him."

Shen considered for a brief moment before nodding slowly.

"Do as you please," Shen said.

The command hung in the air, final and absolute.

Back at the village, Tadanaka gathered his group and quickly gave his instructions. He asked Miji and Satora to remain behind, ordering them to stay and watch over the villagers until he returned. Miji, although reluctant, accepted without question, and both he and Satora nodded firmly, determined to protect the people who had suffered enough.

Meanwhile, Tadanaka, Kume, and Suru set off quietly, trailing the bandit from a distance through the thinning woods. None of them noticed that hidden among the trees, a dark figure watched their every move—a Mutant, cloaked in the forest's shadows, studying them in silence.

Unaware that he was being followed, the bandit made his way into a small, run-down bar tucked into the side of a hill. Inside, the rest of his companions—rough-looking men with hardened faces—were already gathered. As the bandit pushed through the door, the leader of the group, a burly man with a jagged scar across his face, stood up from his seat.

"Where's the money?" the leader demanded, his voice rough and impatient.

The bandit stammered slightly, still nursing the bruises Tadanaka had given him. "Reiki warriors stopped me. They threatened me, told me not to come back."

Hearing this, the leader's face twisted into anger. Without hesitation, he barked at his men to grab their weapons and prepare to storm the village.

Before they could move, the doors of the bar swung open with a hard thud. Tadanaka stepped inside with calm, steady steps, flanked by Kume and Suru, who entered quietly behind him. The air shifted immediately, a heavy tension filling the cramped space.

"Who the hell are you supposed to be?" the leader growled, narrowing his eyes at the young man standing so boldly in front of him.

Tadanaka didn't flinch. His voice was steady, filled with quiet authority. "I'm the one who's going to teach you a lesson for stealing from people who can't even defend themselves."

Recognition lit up the bandit's face, and he pointed at Tadanaka in panic. "It's him! He's the one who beat me up and stopped me from taking the payment!"

Fury surged through the leader, who ordered all his men to attack at once with a violent gesture.

The bandits lunged forward in a wild rush, but they were no match for the disciplined warriors they faced. Kume moved first, disarming the nearest bandit with a swift strike to his wrist, her movements sharp and fluid. Suru, silent and composed as always, countered another attack with a single crushing blow that knocked his opponent to the ground.

Within moments, the floor of the bar was littered with groaning bandits, their weapons scattered uselessly across the floor. Tadanaka stood at the center of it all, his expression cold and focused, already preparing for what was coming.

Tadanaka stepped forward, his boots pressing firmly into the dusty wooden floor as he approached the bandit leader without apprehension.

His hand slid to the hilt of his sword, drawing it with a clean motion and leveling the blade at the man's throat.

His voice rang out, calm but firm, carrying the authority of someone who had seen enough corruption to have no patience left for it. "You have committed crimes against innocent people. You preyed on the weak and helpless. For that, you will answer for your deeds. You are under arrest and will face justice for what you've done," Tadanaka declared, his eyes narrowing with disgust.

The bandit leader, a bulky man with crooked teeth and wild eyes, simply laughed in response. There was no fear in him—only arrogance and something darker beneath his smirk. He straightened his back and, with a sneer, said, "You have no idea who you're dealing with, boy. Lord Gazan will hear about this. He will rain hell down on you and every last villager you think you're protecting. You're not facing just bandits anymore. You're facing the Torima."

At the mention of that name, a visible flicker of tension crossed Tadanaka's face. For a heartbeat, the room itself seemed to grow heavier. The Torima were no ordinary threat—they were among the strongest of the Mutahawls, second only to the Obake themselves. Knowing that these lowlifes were tied to them changed everything.

Still, Tadanaka did not back down. His grip on his sword tightened, his voice low but filled with venom as he answered, "The Torima? You're nothing but a coward hiding behind greater monsters." Without another word, he moved with precision, striking the bandit leader with the hilt of his sword. The man crumpled to the floor, unconscious before he even hit the ground.

Tadanaka sheathed his weapon in a smooth motion and turned sharply to Kume and Suru, who had already secured the other bandits. "We need to move," he said with urgency. "If Gazan hears what happened, he won't just send threats. He'll send death. We need to get back to the village before it's too late."

Back at the village, Miji, Satora, Yasaze, and Shiro were still helping the villagers settle when an unsettling tension spread through the air. Without warning, figures emerged from the distant woods—hulking Mutants, each one exuding menace. At their center walked a tall Mutant, clearly their leader, his eyes sharp and a smug smile playing across his lips. It was Gazan, the Sixth Member of the Torima, surrounded by several of his subordinates. Among them was the same Mutant who had been spying on them earlier; it was he who told Gazan what had been happening in the village.

Miji stepped forward without hesitation, shielding Yasaze and Shiro with his body. "Everyone, get back inside your homes!" he commanded the villagers sharply, his voice cutting through the heavy air. Doors slammed shut and windows were barred within moments, leaving the open ground between the two groups eerily silent.

Miji positioned himself squarely in front of the approaching threat. Satora drew her blade beside him, mirroring his stance. Gazan sauntered closer, his arms loosely folded, the smirk on his face never fading.

GAZAN

"Who are you?" Miji asked, his tone sharp and measured.

Gazan gave a slow, mocking bow. "Good evening, kid," he said with exaggerated politeness. "Name's Gazan. One of my Mutants told me you interfered with our business here. I'm feeling generous tonight, so I'll give you a chance—walk away quietly, and I might pretend this never happened."

Miji's expression hardened. He wasn't interested in talking. He shifted slightly, then leaned toward Satora, speaking low enough so only she could hear. "Satora," he said calmly but firmly, "I'll handle Gazan. You take care of the other Mutants."

Satora gave a small nod, her blade gleaming in the fading light.

Miji then turned his head toward Yasaze and Shiro, who stood frozen behind him. "You two," he said, voice serious and commanding, "hide now. Don't come out no matter what."

Yasaze hesitated for a moment, but Shiro grabbed his hand and together they retreated toward one of the nearby houses, slipping out of sight just as the tension exploded.

Miji unsheathed his blade with a single, fluid motion, leveling it toward Gazan. "We're not leaving," he said. "You picked the wrong village."

Miji and Satora moved without hesitation. Miji charged directly at Gazan, drawing his blade with a fierce determination, while Satora turned her focus to the Mutants that had accompanied him.

Miji unleashed a relentless assault, striking with all the strength and speed he could muster. But it quickly became clear that Gazan was no ordinary opponent. His movements were sharp, his power overwhelming. Every blow Miji landed was either dodged or blocked with ease, while every counterattack from Gazan forced Miji further onto the defensive.

Although Satora fought hard against the Mutants, cutting them down one after another, she could only spare quick, worried glances toward Miji, seeing him struggle to hold his ground against an opponent who fought like an unstoppable force.

Satora gritted her teeth and pushed harder, knowing she had to finish the fight quickly. Still, even after clearing the others, turning her attention to Gazan revealed that Miji was barely holding his ground. Every clash between them sent shockwaves through the earth, and every time their weapons met, it was obvious that Gazan was simply toying with him. Satora rushed to join Miji, striking alongside him with everything she had, but even the two of them together were not enough to bring Gazan down.

Between heavy breaths, Miji realized the situation was rapidly getting worse. If they continued like this, they wouldn't survive, and worse—the villagers, Yasaze, and Shiro would all be in danger. He clenched his jaw and made a decision.

"Satora," Miji said, glancing at her urgently while still holding Gazan at bay, "you have to go. Find Captain Tadanaka and the others. Tell them what's happening—hurry!"

Satora's eyes widened, a mix of fear and refusal flashing across her face. "I won't leave you here!" she shouted back.

"You have to!" Miji barked, his voice hard and commanding. "For the sake of the village. For Yasaze and Shiro. You must go—NOW!"

For a moment, Satora hesitated, torn between her loyalty to her comrade and the greater duty Miji was placing in her hands. But seeing the unyielding determination in Miji's expression, she finally forced herself to act. With one last look at him, she turned and sprinted toward the woods, racing to find Tadanaka and the others.

Miji stayed behind, tightening his grip on his sword as he turned to fully face Gazan. Alone now, he stood between Gazan and the people he had sworn to protect, ready to give everything he had to buy them time.

Out of nowhere, Shiro appeared, her face pale with fear as she stood in the middle of chaos. Her voice shook, but she still shouted out at Gazan to leave the village alone. Miji, caught off guard and filled with panic, immediately yelled at her to run, but it was too late—Gazan had already locked his eyes on Miji as he saw him lose focus, and decisively launched his attack.

Deep in the woods, Tadanaka, Kume, and Suru were rushing back toward the village at full speed when they suddenly encountered Satora sprinting toward them. Breathless but determined, Satora quickly explained everything that had happened—the arrival of Gazan, the battle, and Miji's decision to stay behind and protect everyone. When Tadanaka ordered everyone to move without wasting another second, they raced back to the village with everything they had.

They were greeted by a grim, unsettling sight. Miji was lying on the ground, severely injured and unconscious, his body battered from head to toe. A few steps away, Shiro was also sprawled on the dirt, unconscious and hurt but showing faint signs of life. Gazan, the threat that had terrorized the villagers, lay motionless nearby—dead.

The moment he took in the scene, Tadanaka rushed toward Miji, dropping to his knees beside him, checking desperately for any sign of life. Relief washed over him when he found a pulse, though it was weak.

As he struggled to think of what to do next, a man from among the gathered villagers stepped forward. "I'm a doctor," he said urgently. "Let me take care of him."

Tadanaka immediately bowed his head in gratitude. "Thank you, doctor. I am in your debt," he said, his voice heavy with both relief and worry.

Meanwhile, Kume and Satora had hurried to Shiro's side. As they carefully checked her condition, Shiro's eyes fluttered open. Disoriented and frightened, she tried to sit up, her voice trembling. "What happened?...WHERE IS THE MUTANT?!" she cried out, panic still gripping her.

Kume placed a steadying hand on her shoulder, offering a reassuring smile. "Don't worry," she said softly. "He's dead. You're safe now."

Tadanaka and the rest of the crew stood over the aftermath, confusion tightening around them like a noose. They gathered the villagers, asking urgently if anyone had seen what happened, but each villager shook their head, none of them able to explain how Gazan had been killed. The uncertainty left an uneasy feeling in the air.

Before Tadanaka could press further, Yasaze approached him, his face pale but determined. Tadanaka immediately turned to him, relief flooding his features. "Yasaze! Thank God you're okay. Are you hurt?" he asked, quickly looking him over.

"I'm fine, big brother…but I saw everything," Yasaze said, his voice steady despite the weight of what he had witnessed. Tadanaka crouched slightly to meet his eyes, urging him to continue.

"Gazan defeated Miji and knocked out Shiro. Just as he was about to kill them both, a warrior appeared out of nowhere and struck Gazan down," Yasaze explained, still trying to process it himself.

"A warrior?" Tadanaka repeated, his brows contracting in concern. "Who was it? Did you recognize him?"

Yasaze shook his head. "No, I didn't. I've never seen him before."

Forcing himself to stay focused, Tadanaka took a breath. "We'll figure it out later. For now, we need to make sure Miji recovers," he said firmly.

Once the doctor had finished treating Miji's wounds and stabilized his condition, Shiro quietly excused herself and left the village. The rest of the group, weary but determined, made their way back to the Gochuu base, carrying Miji carefully with them. Upon arrival, Tadanaka gave a final order before heading out.

"Stay by Miji's side and make sure he rests. I'll report what happened to Master Yuuta," he said, setting off toward the main castle without another word.

Tadanaka made his way to the main castle, his steps quick and purposeful despite the exhaustion weighing on him. Upon arriving, he was immediately granted an audience with Master Yuuta. Tadanaka bowed respectfully and immediately began to explain everything that had transpired at the village— the bandits' involvement, their connection to the Torima, and how he had ordered warriors to capture the remaining bandits and place them under arrest.

As he spoke, Yuuta listened carefully, his expression calm but serious. When Tadanaka described the part about Gazan's unexpected defeat, Yuuta leaned slightly forward, his voice even. "Yasaze couldn't identify the warrior who defeated Gazan?" he asked.

Tadanaka shook his head. "No, Master. Yasaze didn't recognize him. But we will find out who he is soon enough."

Yuuta's eyes narrowed slightly in thought. "The Torima have been making bold moves lately. Their activity is increasing."

He sat back, considering the situation for a moment before speaking again. "I will make sure to bring this up the day after tomorrow during the meeting with the Haras."

Tadanaka's eyebrows lifted slightly at that. "The meeting with the Haras...it's the day after tomorrow?" he asked, surprised.

"Yes," Yuuta confirmed with a nod. "We'll discuss the necessary precautions then."

CHAPTER FOURTEEN
Summon the Nokuba

Deep within the woods, as two Reiki warriors were patrolling the woods they found themselves face to face with a chilling figure cloaked in dark power. Nobu, the Fifth Member of the Obake, stood before them, his presence alone so oppressive that the warriors struggled to keep their footing. The air around him seemed heavier, thicker; despite their instincts screaming at them to act, they dropped to their knees under the sheer weight of his Dark Reiki.

A twisted smile curled across Nobu's face as he regarded them almost playfully. "Hey, hey, no need to get so worked up," he said, his voice light but dripping with malice. "Don't worry. I'm not here to kill you... at least, not both of you. Let's play a game. Pick a number between one and ten."

The warriors exchanged a desperate glance but said nothing, their bodies frozen by the overwhelming aura pouring from Nobu. His smile widened, his tone sharpening. "If you don't choose, I'll kill you both right now."

Cornered, they quickly blurted out their choices—one said six, the other said two. Nobu's eyes gleamed with amusement. "Oh, you picked six. That's close. I chose seven, so...congratulations, you live." His voice darkened as he turned to the second warrior. "But you, unlucky number two—you lose."

Nobu's hand moved. The second warrior's head was severed cleanly from his body, the act so swift and casual it was as if he were brushing away an insect. Blood stained the ground as the surviving trembled in horror, unable to process what had just happened.

Nobu crouched down beside the fallen head and, with a sinister calmness, rolled it toward the remaining warrior. "Be a good boy," Nobu said, his voice almost cheerful, "and deliver a message for me. Take your friend's head and bring it straight to your Lord Ryoze. Tell him..." he leaned in slightly, his smile growing wider, "...that I'm coming for him very soon."

The surviving warrior, paralyzed by fear, could do nothing but nod as Nobu stood tall again, his dark aura swirling around him like a living nightmare.

At Ryoze's castle, the evening had been calm. Naru moved quietly across the room, serving tea to Ryoze as he sat by the low table, glancing over a few reports that had arrived earlier from the Toukan province. The stillness was interrupted when one of the castle guards approached in a hurry, bowing respectfully at the entrance before speaking.

"Lord Ryoze, a Reiki warrior requests an audience with you. He says it's urgent."

Ryoze set down his cup without hesitation and gave a small nod. "Allow him to enter."

The door was opened wider, and the warrior stepped inside. His clothes were bloodstained, and it was clear from the tremble in his body that he had seen something terrible. Ryoze, calm as ever, offered him a slight smile to ease the tension. "It's alright," he said, his voice steady. "Tell me what happened."

The warrior struggled to steady himself but finally pulled something from the cloth he carried. Gasps filled the room when he revealed it—the severed head of another Reiki warrior. Blood still stained the dead man's features, frozen in a final expression of shock.

"We were attacked," the trembling warrior said, his voice barely above a whisper. "By Nobu...a Member of the Obake."

At the mention of the Obake, both Ryoze and Naru tensed. Their expressions darkened immediately. Even for seasoned warriors like them, the Obake were not names to be taken lightly.

The warrior continued, forcing the words out despite the fear gripping him. "He decapitated my companion and...he spared me only to deliver a message. He said to tell you...that he is coming for you."

There was a heavy silence in the room as the weight of the words settled in. Ryoze rose slowly to his feet, his eyes unreadable. He stepped toward the warrior and placed a hand briefly on his shoulder. "You did well to deliver this message," Ryoze said calmly. "You may leave now. Get some rest."

The warrior bowed, grateful, and hurried out of the chamber.

For a long moment, Ryoze said nothing. He stood staring out toward the far wall, his mind deep in thought. Naru remained quiet as well, waiting. Finally, Ryoze's low and certain voice broke the silence.

"So...the Obake are on the move."

Naru looked at him seriously. "What should we do, Lord?"

Another pause. Then, with a calmness that carried the full weight of his resolve, Ryoze answered, "Summon the Members of the Nokuba."

Naru bowed slightly, her voice unwavering. "Understood, Lord."

Without another word, she turned and swiftly moved to carry out the order, while Ryoze remained behind, already preparing for the battle that he knew was soon to come.

High in the mountains, the air sharp and thin, a lone Reiki warrior stood amidst the remains of fallen Mutants. With his blade dripping with the last traces of battle, he calmly wiped it clean on the torn cloth of one of the defeated creatures. His sharp eyes swept across the rocky clearing, silently counting the bodies of the Mutants he killed.

It had been a long hunt, but a necessary one. These stronger Mutants were growing bolder, and Mizo Abahare made it his personal duty to hunt them down before they could threaten the nearby villages.

As he finished his count, his senses sharpened—someone was approaching. Without hesitation, Mizo turned to see a single figure carefully making his way through the uneven terrain. The man wore the insignia of the Toukan Clan, a clear sign that he was an official messenger.

The messenger bowed respectfully. "Lord Mizo," he said, his voice steady despite the rough climb. "You have been summoned by Lord Ryoze."

Mizo slid his blade back into its sheath without a word, his expression calm but serious. He gave a small nod of acknowledgment. "Understood."

This was no ordinary summons. Mizo knew Ryoze Toukan well enough to understand that if he was being called back personally, something important was about to unfold.

Without wasting another breath, Mizo turned and began descending the mountain path, the wind tugging at his cloak. He was Mizo Abahare—heir of the Abahare Clan and the Fifth-ranked Member of the Nokuba—and when duty called, he was always ready.

Mizo Abahare

In the southeastern region of Alard, within the heart of the Laitonn Clan's castle, a young woman sat quietly in a sunlit chamber, her hand moving gracefully across a parchment. Brush in hand, she worked on a delicate painting, her face calm and her silver-white hair falling softly around her shoulders. The world outside the castle walls seemed distant as she lost herself in her art, the strokes of her brush full of life and careful attention.

The moment of peace was interrupted when the doors slid open and footsteps echoed into the room. Without needing to look up, she sensed that whoever had entered carried a different kind of presence—formal, heavy with urgency. When she lifted her eyes, her smile faded instantly.

Standing before her was a messenger wearing the unmistakable insignia of the Toukan Clan.

He bowed respectfully. "Lord Ina, you have been summoned by Lord Ryoze," he announced.

Ina set her brush down carefully, wiping her hands on a cloth as she rose to her feet. Her expression, once bright and serene, had shifted to something more serious and composed. "Understood," she replied immediately.

This was no casual summons. She knew there was a meaning behind a call from Ryoze Toukan.

Ina Laitonn—the Fourth-ranked Member of the Nokuba and heir to the Laitonn Clan—gave one last glance at her unfinished painting before turning to make her way to meet Lord Ryoze. Whatever awaited her now was far more important than the quiet life she often longed for.

INA LAITONN

At a lively bar in the center of town, laughter and music filled the air. Three men sat around a table cluttered with empty cups, surrounded by a few women who giggled at their jokes. At the center of it all was Mado, a man laughing so hard that he nearly spilled his drink.

"You've already had more than ten cups, Mado!" one of the men teased, raising his own cup with a wide grin.

Mado laughed even louder, slapping the table with the palm of his hand. "Of course! I've got to impress these lovely ladies. We're having too much fun to stop now!" he said, tossing another drink back and motioning for the waitress. "Keep the drinks coming!" he called out, drawing more laughter from the group.

The atmosphere was light and carefree—until a man in formal robes pushed open the door and entered the bar, wearing the Toukan Clan's insignia. The messenger approached the table with a serious expression, his presence casting a sudden chill over the room.

Mado looked up at him, squinting drunkenly. "Why do you look so serious, dummy? Come on, have a drink with us," Mado said to the messenger, laughing again. His companions, clearly drunk, burst into laughter as well.

The messenger, undeterred, bowed slightly. "Lord Mado, you have been summoned by Lord Ryoze," he said.

The effect was immediate. Mado's laughter stopped, his drunken expression sharpening into a cold, sober seriousness. The weight of the name 'Ryoze' was not something he took lightly.

One of the drunken men beside him, oblivious to the change in mood, scoffed and slurred, "Who does this Ryoze think he is, an idiot trying to ruin the fun? Tell him to—"

Before he could finish, Mado grabbed the man's head with one hand and slammed it hard against the wooden table, the sound echoing through the bar. The women screamed and backed away.

"If you disrespect Lord Ryoze again," Mado said, his voice low and deadly, "I'll have your head."

The bar fell into silence. No one dared move.

Mado turned back to the messenger, his tone now respectful and steady. "Understood," he said firmly.

Without another word, he pushed himself up from the table, adjusted himself, and headed out into the night.

Mado—the Third-ranked Member of the Nokuba—had been summoned.

MADO

CHAPTER FIFTEEN
Unmasked

Shiro moved quietly along a narrow path in the woods, her steps steady and unhurried. The trees stretched above her, but she paid no mind to their gently swaying branches. Her attention was elsewhere, lost in her own thoughts.

Without warning, four Mutants emerged from the trees ahead, blocking her path. They stood with wicked grins, each one sizing her up like a prize. One of them, larger than the others, stepped forward.

"Well, well…if it isn't a lovely lady walking all by herself," he said with a sneer. "The first one to kill her gets her Reiki."

The others laughed, their dark energy already flaring up in anticipation.

But Shiro didn't even react. She kept walking without a glance, completely unfazed, as if the four of them weren't even worth her attention.

Enraged by her lack of fear, all four Mutants attacked her at once, their claws flashing as they rushed her.

Shiro finally came to a stop.

With one smooth and easy motion, she raised her arm and swung it across in front of her.

A wave of energy burst out in an instant, too fast for the Mutants to react. Before they even realized what had happened, they all collapsed to the ground—killed in a single move.

Shiro stood quietly, looking down at their fallen bodies without a hint of emotion.

Suddenly a strange, puzzled look crossed her face.

"Have my Reiki?" she muttered to herself. "What the hell were those fools talking about?"

She lifted her hands and stared at them. They looked just like any normal human hands. That's when she noticed it.

"Ah...I'm still in my human form," she said quietly.

Calmly, Shiro's body began to change. Dark Reiki started to swirl around her as she began to change, revealing her true nature.

In just a few seconds, the disguise was gone.

Standing there now wasn't the helpless, kind-hearted Shiro, the soft-spoken girl everyone believed her to be.

She was something far more dangerous.

She had never been human to begin with. She was a Mutant all along—but not just any Mutant.

She was Laya, the Fourth Member of the Obake—one of the five strongest beings among the Mutahawls, a force whose very presence could silence entire armies.

LAYA

Laya. A name that, when spoken aloud, made even the boldest warriors hesitate.

But a chilling question hung in the air.

Why would a Mutant as powerful as Laya choose to disguise herself among humans?

CHAPTER SIXTEEN
The Circle of Six

Meanwhile, the Members of the Nokuba had gathered outside Ryoze's castle, each arriving from different corners of the land. Mizo, never one to hide his excitement, threw his arms into the air and called out with a wide grin, "Hey, guys! It's been a while—I missed you all!"

Mado crossed his arms and rolled his eyes, giving a tired sigh. "Shut the hell up. Looks like you're still as damn loud as ever," he muttered, though a faint smirk tugged at the corner of his mouth.

Ina approached with a gentle smile, her white hair flowing softly behind her. "It's good to see you, Mizo. Have you been well?" she asked warmly.

Before Mizo could launch into another noisy reply, Naru stepped out from the entrance of the castle, her calm and commanding presence immediately drawing their attention. As the wife of Lord Ryoze—co-leader of the Nokuba and the one ranked second among its Members—she held a position of great respect and authority. Without needing to speak a word, all the gathered Nokuba Members straightened their backs and bowed respectfully, a silent acknowledgment not only of her connection to their leader, but also of her own strength and standing within the Nokuba.

They all walked into Ryoze's chamber in a calm, respectful line, standing side by side. The Nokuba Members immediately knelt before their leader, heads bowed low. The unflappable Ina was the first to speak, her voice clear and warm.

"Lord Ryoze, it gladdens me to see that you are in good health," she said with genuine respect.

Mado, usually loud and carefree, set aside his wild nature the moment he stepped forward. His voice carried no trace of his typical laughter or teasing, only a rare seriousness that showed the depth of his loyalty. "I came immediately after receiving your summons, my Lord," he said, bowing his head lower in respect. "I await your command." There was no need for him to act tough or put on a show; in the presence of Ryoze, Mado's loyalty spoke louder than words.

Meanwhile, Mizo stayed kneeling, feeling a drop of sweat slide down his face. As he listened to the others speak so respectfully, he realized with panic that he hadn't prepared anything to say. *"Damn it…they all said something cool and respectful while I was sitting here wondering if I was in trouble. I'm such an idiot,"* he thought. He kept his head low, hoping no one noticed how awkward he felt.

Ryoze looked over them all, a faint smile on his lips, recognizing both their loyalty and Mizo's unspoken panic. "It's good seeing you all here," Ryoze finally said, his voice calm and reassuring. "I hope you've been doing well—and staying out of trouble."

The atmosphere lightened for a moment before Ryoze's tone shifted slightly, more serious now. "I have summoned you all because there has been a recent increase in activity from the Torima…and the Obake."

The moment the word "Obake" left Ryoze's lips, all the Nokuba Members instinctively lifted their heads and looked at him, their expressions sharpening with tension.

"The Obake?" they said almost in unison, the name alone enough to stir a deep unease among even the strongest.

"Yes," Ryoze confirmed, his gaze steady, already preparing to deliver the news none of them would take lightly.

At the Gochuu base, Miji was finally back on his feet, his injuries mostly healed. Tadanaka sat across from him, eager to hear anything he could remember about the attack. Miji lowered his head slightly, trying to piece together the fragmented memories. "My memory is faded for some reason," he admitted, his voice heavy with frustration, "but I remember Gazan being extremely powerful…and I thought I was going to die. That's all I can recall."

Before Tadanaka could say anything more, Suru entered the room quietly. "Captain Tadanaka, there is a messenger here for you," Suru announced. Tadanaka stood and followed him outside, where a young man wearing the Toukan insignia was waiting.

"Lord Tadanaka, you and the Members of the Gochuu have been summoned by Lord Ryoze," the messenger said respectfully.

Hearing his brother's name, a troubled look crossed Tadanaka's face. His mind immediately filled with questions, but he kept his composure. "Big brother?...Understood," he said, his voice steady despite the unease growing inside him. Turning back toward the base, he called out with firm authority, "Everyone gather immediately! We leave for Lord Ryoze's castle at once!"

The Gochuu Members reached their destination, stepping inside his chamber after being granted permission. As they entered, their eyes were immediately drawn to the sight before them. Lord Ryoze sat at the center, calm and composed, with Mado and Ina seated to his left and Naru and Mizo to his right. Their strong combined presence filled the room with heavy pressure. The strength coming from the Nokuba was clear, weighing heavily on the Gochuu Members even without trying. Tadanaka and the others dropped to one knee, showing Lord Ryoze their full respect by bowing low before him.

"Thank you for coming, everyone," Ryoze said, his voice calm yet carrying undeniable authority. "I have gathered both you and the Nokuba to discuss important matters."

Kume remained silent, her gaze shifting toward the figures surrounding Ryoze. She could feel it without question—the strength they carried was real. These were the Nokuba, the warriors she had only heard about in stories. Now, seeing them with her own eyes, she finally understood why their names were spoken with such respect and fear across the land.

"Tadanaka, Kume," Ryoze called out.

"YES, LORD!" they answered in unison, still kneeling.

"You will be led by Mado and Ina," Ryoze continued. "Your mission is to hunt down and slay Roka, the Fourth Member of the Torima, and Kanaja, the Fifth Member."

At his next call, "Suru, Satora, Miji," the three remaining Gochuu Members answered immediately, their voices sharp and clear as they remained kneeling. "You will be under the command of Mizo," Ryoze said, his gaze shifting slightly to the Fifth Member of the Nokuba. "Your mission is to search for any traces of the Obake. However, if you encounter any of them, you are not to engage. You are not ready to face an Obake in battle."

"Understood, Lord!" they replied in unison, their heads bowed lower, acknowledging the gravity of their orders.

Ryoze paused for a moment, letting the weight of his words settle. Then his tone grew stronger. "It is time for us to make our move. We will not sit silently and allow them to strike at us first. Now is the time to act—and we will strike first."

"YES, MY LORD!" the Nokuba and Gochuu answered together, their voices firm and united as they bowed once more.

Satisfied, Ryoze gave them one last look before straightening his posture. "Alright. I must leave now or I'll be late for the Haras meeting," he said simply, and without another word, got up and left the chamber.

At the main castle, many Reiki warriors had gathered at the front gates. Today was a ceremony to welcome the Members of the Haras. Ryoze arrived at the castle and was quickly joined by Shita near the entrance.

"Ryoze, it's nice to see you," Shita said with a slight smile.

"You too, Shita. Have the Haras Members arrived yet?" Ryoze asked, glancing around.

"They'll be here any minute…Speak of the devil, here they are," Shita replied, her voice shifting to a more serious tone.

The gathered warriors erupted into respectful cheers as three figures began walking steadily toward the castle's main gate.

The first was Mayu Abahare, one of the Haras and the leader of the Abahare Clan—known throughout Alard as the Water Lord. At her side was Baraqu Laitonn, leader of the Laitonn Clan and known as the Lightning Lord. Walking beside him was Lahab Akaryu, fierce leader of the Akaryu Clan, titled the Fire Lord.

LAHAB AKARYU

BARAQU LAITONN

MAYU ABAHARE

The room carried a heavy, undeniable weight—here sat all six people alive who had awakened their Reiki. The air itself seemed to grow thicker under the immense spiritual presence gathered within those walls.

These three leaders were not only the heads of their clans, but also among the rare few who had awakened their Reiki. Each of them had been entrusted with guarding one of the four glass plates, artifacts tied directly to the sealing of the Mutotsu.

The Haras Members reached the gates and were respectfully welcomed by Shita and Ryoze. The three leaders promptly bowed to them, acknowledging Ryoze's and Shita's authority.

"Lord Ryoze, Lord Shita, it's been a while," Lahab said warmly.

"Welcome, everyone. Follow me; let's not keep Master Yuuta waiting any longer," Ryoze replied, his voice steady and formal.

Together, Ryoze, Shita, and the Members of the Haras entered the main hall and made their way to Yuuta's chamber. Upon entering, everyone immediately kneeled before Yuuta. Ryoze alone rose after kneeling, taking his place by Yuuta's side as the others sat respectfully before their ruler.

Yuuta welcomed them with a calm smile and asked about their wellbeing.

"Master Yuuta, I hope you are doing well," Baraqu said respectfully.

"How are things in your provinces? I trust there is no trouble?" Yuuta asked.

"We eliminate Mutants daily to maintain peace and make sure your laws are being followed," Mayu replied confidently.

"With you as our ruler, no one dares cause trouble," Lahab added.

"That's good to hear. But we need to discuss urgent matters. There has been increased movement from the Torima lately, and more troubling, Nobu of the Obake has appeared and made a threat toward Ryoze," Yuuta said, his voice deepening.

"The Obake?!" Baraqu exclaimed, his eyes narrowing.

"Nobu, you say?!" Mayu echoed, her voice filled with anger.

"Yes. He decapitated one of our Reiki warriors and sent the head as a message to Ryoze," Yuuta said grimly. "You should also know that we have already defeated and killed three Members of the Torima. I have sent the Nokuba and the Gochuu Members on missions to eliminate two more." Ryoze added.

"That is good to hear. Then I will leave the matter of the Torima to you, Ryoze," Yuuta said firmly.

"Yes, my Lord," Ryoze answered, bowing his head slightly.

Yuuta's tone grew even sharper. "From now on, we must be on high alert. The Mutants already possess one of the four glass plates. We cannot afford to lose another. Lahab, Baraqu, Mayu—you are to keep your provinces under constant surveillance. If anything suspicious occurs, you are to report to me immediately. Is that understood?"

"Understood, Lord!" the three Haras leaders replied in unison.

CHAPTER SEVENTEEN
The Weight of What's Left Behind

With that, the meeting ended and the leaders filed out of Yuuta's chamber, each one carrying the weight of the future on their shoulders.

Ryoze was walking back toward his castle when he heard a voice call out from behind him.

"Lord Ryoze, please wait," Mayu said as she rushed to catch up. He stopped and turned slightly, his expression calm as he looked at her.

"What is it, Mayu?" he asked.

Without hesitation, Mayu dropped to her knees before him, lowering her head to the ground.

"Lord Ryoze, Nobu has finally shown himself," she said, her voice trembling with urgency. "Please allow me to go after him."

Ryoze narrowed his eyes slightly but answered in a composed tone. "No. You are a Member of the Haras now. You have a duty to—" he began, but Mayu quickly interrupted, lifting her head to meet his gaze with desperation burning in her eyes.

"The plate entrusted to the Abahare family was taken," she said sharply. "It's already in the hands of the Mutants. I have nothing left to protect as a Haras Member."

Ryoze's expression hardened, but he answered firmly.

"Even so, your duty is not just the plate. As the leader of the Abahare Clan, you must protect your lands and make sure the Mutants do not cause chaos there."

Mayu's hands trembled as she clenched her fists against the dirt. Tears welled up in her eyes, but she forced herself to speak clearly.

"Lord Ryoze…the only reason I even became a Haras Member was because it was your wish," she said. "When I served under you in the Nokuba, you gave us freedom. You allowed us to roam free. But now, as a Haras Member, I am obligated to protect my lands and cannot leave my region. Please…" Her voice broke as tears rolled down her cheeks. "Please take me back."

Ryoze stared at her for a long moment, his face unreadable. Then, without saying anything more, he turned his back to her and began walking away.

"No," he said coldly, his voice cutting through the silence like a blade. His steps did not slow, and he did not look back.

Mayu remained kneeling on the ground, her body shaking with sobs as she watched him walk away. She pressed her forehead against the dirt, the pain in her chest growing heavier by the second. In the stillness that followed, her mind flooded with memories—of her past and what lay behind her anger and sorrow.

Four years ago...

In the lands of the Abahare Clan, the sun was just beginning to rise over the main castle. Inside, the usual quiet was broken by hurried footsteps and familiar voices.

"Come on, Mayu. Lord Ryoze summoned us—we're going to be late," Ina called from the entrance.

Mayu Abahare was the Third-ranked Member of the Nokuba. She moved quickly through the hall, already running late.

Mizo stepped out from behind one of the columns. He was Mayu's younger brother by only a year, and though not yet part of the Nokuba at the time, his strength and discipline were already clear.

"Just wait," he added with a confident smirk. "I'll be joining the Nokuba soon enough."

Mayu looked over her shoulder and gave him a half-smile, arms crossing loosely in front of her.

"Keep training hard," she replied. "Maybe then you'll catch up to me."

Mizo let out a short laugh and nodded. "I'm not far behind, you know."

Before Mayu could respond, a gentle voice came from the doorway behind them.

"Take care, dear. And make sure you come back in time for dinner," their mother said warmly.

MOYA ABAHARE

Moya Abahare was the leader of the Abahare Clan and one of the three current Members of the Haras. She was the most powerful Reiki warrior in the Abahare Clan, also entrusted with one of the four glass plates. Despite her high position and heavy responsibilities, she remained a caring mother to her two children, Mayu and Mizo.

"I will, Mother," Mayu said, her smile softening.

With that, she turned and followed Ina and Naru out of the castle grounds. The three of them moved quickly, heading toward Ryoze's castle. They entered Ryoze's chamber and bowed respectfully. Ryoze stood near the center of the room, his expression serious as he addressed them.

"There have been reports of deaths in a village," he began. "When we sent Reiki warriors to investigate, most of them were either killed or disappeared. Normally, a case like this wouldn't be given to the Nokuba, but we can't afford to lose more warriors. I know this may seem like a small mission, but we must protect the people and the land—no matter the scale of the threat. Will you take care of it?"

Ina stepped forward. "Our sword is yours."

Mayu nodded. "We are under your command."

Naru, standing beside her teammates, gave Ryoze, her husband, a warm smile. "We'll take care of it, my Lord."

Ryoze gave a short nod. "Thank you. Then I leave it to you. Good luck."

Naru, Ina, and Mayu crouched just outside the village, carefully observing from a distance. The sky had darkened, and the village below was quiet. Too quiet. They remained alert, waiting for any sign of Mutant movement.

Mayu let out a quiet sigh. "Mom is going to kill me. It's already night-time, and I promised I'd be back in time for dinner."

Ina, still watching the village, replied calmly, "Lord Ryoze gave us this mission. There's nothing we can do. I'm sure she'll understand."

Naru glanced at Mayu and smirked. "Can't blame her. I'd be terrified too if Lord Moya was my mother."

The three of them laughed softly. For a brief moment, the tension faded.

Suddenly, a sharp scream pierced the air. It was a child's voice, coming from inside the village. The laughter stopped immediately. Without hesitation, they rushed toward the sound.

When they arrived, they found seven Mutants gathered in the village square. One of them had a small girl in his grasp, choking her with one hand. Naru moved without a word, her blade flashing as she charged forward. She sliced through the Mutant's arm, catching the girl before she could fall. Holding the child tightly, she looked back.

"Mayu, Ina—now!" she shouted.

Mayu and Ina moved in unison. With quick, precise strikes, they cut through the remaining Mutants. The fight was over in seconds. The creatures didn't stand a chance.

Once the area was clear, Naru returned the little girl to her frightened parents, who thanked her repeatedly through their tears. She gave them a reassuring nod before turning back to her team.

"Alright, let's go report back to Lord Ryoze," Ina said.

"It's fine," Naru replied. "You both can head home. I'll handle the report."

"You're the best, Naru! Thank you!" Mayu said cheerfully as she started running off toward the Abahare castle.

Ina gave a small wave and began heading toward the Laitonn region.

Naru stayed behind for a moment, watching them go before turning toward Ryoze's castle to deliver the report to her husband herself.

As Mayu hurried back toward the Abahare castle, she heard screams echoing from inside the walls. Her heart dropped. Without thinking, she sprinted toward the main entrance.

When she arrived, she found Mizo standing near the gate, frozen in shock. She rushed over to him.

"Mizo! What's happening?" she asked urgently.

Mizo turned to her, his face pale and his body shaking. "He took the plate," he said, his voice filled with fear. "He was too strong. I had to run away."

"Who are you talking about?" Mayu demanded.

Before Mizo could answer, a calm but chilling voice cut through the air.

"Well, hello, kids," Nobu said as he approached, a group of Mutants following close behind. His steps were slow and relaxed, but the pressure he carried was crushing. Every instinct in Mayu and Mizo's bodies screamed at them to run. It wasn't just the sight of him—it was the feeling.

An Obake Member stood before them, and the difference between him and ordinary Mutants was impossible to ignore. His presence alone made it hard to breathe. His smile looked casual, but the killing intent surrounding him was heavy and real.

"My apologies," Nobu continued, his tone almost playful. "Since I couldn't find the Haras Member, I'll have to kill one of you instead."

Mayu and Mizo froze. Even standing together, they could feel the pressure coming from Nobu's presence. Neither of them could move.

In the blink of an eye, Nobu attacked, moving with terrifying speed. But just before his strike could land, it was blocked by a powerful force. Moya Abahare stood between them, her expression fierce and unwavering. "I'm sorry I'm late," Moya said quickly. "Mayu, take your brother and get out of here!"

"So Mommy came to the rescue," Nobu said mockingly, tilting his head. "That's cute."

Moya ignored his words. She released her Reiki without holding back, her power exploding outward and shaking the ground beneath them. The air around her grew heavy, and for the first time, Nobu's smile faded.

Nobu quickly realized that Moya was no ordinary opponent. The force of her power left no doubt—she was one of the rare few who had awakened their Reiki. Underestimating her even for a moment would cost him his life.

They clashed without wasting another second, Nobu now fighting seriously as the battle began.

Meanwhile, back at Ryoze's castle, Naru entered the main hall and walked over to where Ryoze was seated. Without hesitation, she sat beside him. Ryoze smiled and hugged her briefly.

"How did the mission go?" he asked.

Before Naru could answer, Ryoze's expression suddenly changed. His face grew serious as he turned his head slightly, sensing something distant but unmistakable. Moya's Reiki had been released—and not just partially, but at full strength.

Ryoze immediately understood what that meant. Moya was one of the rare few who had awakened their Reiki. If she was forced to unleash her full power, then the opponent she faced was not ordinary. It was someone dangerous enough to threaten even a Haras Member.

Without wasting another second, Ryoze stood up and rushed out of the castle, heading straight toward the Abahare main castle. Naru, confused but sensing the urgency, quickly followed after him.

At the Abahare castle, the battle raged on.

"I told you both to get out of here! Leave this to me!" Moya shouted at her children, her voice cutting through the noise.

Mizo stood frozen, unable to move. The fear and pressure from Nobu's presence had left him paralyzed. Seeing this, Mayu grabbed him by the arm and tried to drag him away. But before they could escape, the Mutants under Nobu's command moved in to attack.

Mayu quickly pushed Mizo behind her, fighting off the Mutants with fierce strikes. As she fought, she shouted at her brother, "Run! I'll catch up!"

Mizo hesitated, unable to respond. One of the Mutants slipped past Mayu's defense and rushed toward him. Though Mizo was strong enough to handle the Mutant, the overwhelming fear of Nobu had taken over. He couldn't move.

Seeing the danger, Mayu screamed his name and threw herself between them, cutting the Mutant down just in time. She turned to Mizo, shaking him, her voice trembling. "Mizo! Snap out of it!"

Hearing Mayu's desperate scream, Moya turned her head for just a moment to look at her children. In that brief instant, she lowered her guard.

"It was a mistake to let your guard down, Haras," Nobu said coldly.

In one swift movement, he slashed her across the side, delivering a deep and deadly blow. Moya staggered, blood pouring from the wound as she fell to her knees.

Struggling to speak, she looked at her children and forced out the words, "Run...please..."

Mayu froze in shock, her eyes filling with tears. But knowing they had no choice, she quickly lifted Mizo and ran, her heart breaking with every step as she left her mother behind.

"Not so fast. You're not going anywhere," Nobu said, his voice calm but filled with menace.

Before Mayu could react, she heard the sound of rushing wind. She turned around—and what she saw made her heart stop.

Nobu was already in the air, flying toward them with killing intent clear in his eyes. Mayu froze, still carrying Mizo, but she knew she couldn't outrun him. In that moment, she felt completely helpless. She couldn't move, couldn't fight back. She could only watch as death closed in.

Just as Nobu's strike was about to land, a blur of movement cut across Mayu's vision. Moya appeared in front of them, her body shielding her children without hesitation. Nobu's arm drove forward, piercing straight through Moya's stomach.

Time seemed to freeze.

Mayu and Mizo stared at their mother in horror, unable to comprehend what had just happened. Blood spilled freely from the wound, staining Moya's clothes, but her eyes stayed locked on her children.

Even as pain twisted her face, she forced herself to stand between them and death.

"Go..." Moya gasped, her voice raw and broken.

Tears blurred Mayu's vision. She closed her eyes tightly, clenching her teeth to keep herself from screaming. With every ounce of strength she had left, she turned and ran, carrying Mizo in her arms. She didn't look back. She couldn't.

The farther she ran, the harder it became to breathe. Her chest felt like it was being crushed. Her legs shook with every step. She could hear her own sobs choking in her throat, but she didn't stop. Her mind kept replaying the image of her mother—standing there, wounded and bleeding, protecting them even as her life slipped away.

Her foot caught on something and she stumbled, crashing to the ground. Mizo fell beside her, but she barely noticed. Gasping for air, Mayu pressed her hands into the dirt, trying to force herself to move, but her body wouldn't listen. The shock was too much. The pain in her chest was overwhelming.

Then something inside her broke.

A surge of power exploded from within her. The ground beneath her trembled slightly as her Reiki, dormant until now, finally awakened.

Mayu's breathing grew heavy and deep, a burning rage filling every part of her.

Slowly, she stood up. Her hands were clenched into fists, her arms trembling— not from fear, but from the sheer force of her emotions. Her face, once frozen in panic, was now hardened with fury.

She looked down at Mizo, who was still sitting helplessly on the ground, staring at her with wide, frightened eyes.

"Stay here," Mayu said, her voice low and shaking with anger.

Without waiting for a response, she turned and began walking back toward the battlefield. Each step was heavy, but steady. She no longer felt afraid. There was only one thing left inside her now.

She was going to face Nobu.

Mayu walked steadily toward Nobu, her eyes locked onto him with pure hatred.

"Stupid girl," Nobu said as he watched her approach. His voice was still calm, but it contained a hint of annoyance now. "I was planning to spare you. But if you insist, I'll just send you to your mother."

Mayu said nothing. Her silence was more threatening than any words. The anger and grief burning inside her exploded outward as she released her full Reiki for the first time. The force of it pushed against the air, and Nobu's eyes narrowed.

He immediately realized something had changed. This wasn't the same girl from moments ago. She had awakened her Reiki—and she was far stronger than before.

Before Nobu could decide what to do, several Abahare Reiki warriors arrived, surrounding the area. Seeing the situation turn against him, Nobu clicked his tongue in frustration. He knew staying any longer would be a mistake.

Without another word, he turned and fled into the darkness, disappearing from sight.

As the threat vanished, Mayu's attention dropped back to where her mother lay. She ran toward the body, falling to her knees beside Moya. Her hands trembled as she lifted her mother's lifeless body into her arms. She hugged her tightly, her tears falling freely now.

A moment later, Ryoze and Naru arrived. They stopped at the edge of the broken courtyard, their eyes immediately taking in the scene before them— Mayu crying over Moya's body.

Ryoze's face hardened, but he lowered his head, mourning silently. He didn't need anyone to explain what had happened. He understood it all in a single glance.

Naru, unable to hold back her emotions, walked slowly toward Mayu. She knelt beside her and pulled her into a gentle hug.

Mayu lifted her head slightly, her vision blurred by tears. When she saw Ryoze standing there, she quickly wiped her face with her sleeve, forcing herself to push the emotions back. She didn't want to appear weak in front of her leader. Steadying her breathing, she bowed deeply to him, showing her respect and loyalty.

Ryoze stepped forward and knelt beside her. He placed a hand on her shoulder and lowered his head.

"Mayu..." he said quietly. "I'm sorry I couldn't make it in time. Forgive me."

Mayu stayed silent, clenching her jaw, fighting back the urge to break down again.

Ryoze's voice softened even more. "It's fine. Cry."

Without waiting for a response, Ryoze stood up and turned away, giving her the space to grieve.

The moment he walked away, Mayu could no longer hold it in. She broke down completely, sobbing uncontrollably into Naru's arms, the weight of the loss finally crashing down on her.

At the funeral, the air was heavy with silence. The people of the Abahare Clan stood gathered in mourning, the loss of their leader weighing heavily on everyone's hearts.

Yuuta Toukan stepped forward, his presence commanding but gentle. He walked up to Mayu and Mizo, who immediately bowed low before him.

"I am sorry for your loss," Yuuta said, his voice calm but filled with respect.

"Your mother was a great woman. A true protector of this land."

Mayu kept her head lowered, her hands trembling slightly. "We are sorry for losing the plate...and for letting you down," she said, her voice strained with guilt.

Yuuta shook his head firmly. "The plate is important, but your mother's life was far greater. You did everything you could."

He placed a reassuring hand on Mayu's shoulder.

"I promise you," Yuuta said, his tone sharpening slightly, "she will be avenged."

Later that day, at the Toukan main castle, Yuuta sat alone in his chamber, deep in thought. The weight of recent events hung heavily in the air. The door slid opened quietly, and Ryoze stepped inside. He walked forward and bowed deeply before his father.

"Father," Ryoze said. "I need to ask you for a favor."

Yuuta looked up, his expression calm but concerned. "Is everything alright, son?"

Ryoze straightened, though his eyes showed the guilt he still carried. "I'm asking you to make Mayu a Member of the Haras."

Yuuta didn't respond right away, waiting for his son to explain.

"Becoming a Haras would tie her to the Abahare district," Ryoze continued. "She would be obligated to stay and protect it. I know what kind of freedom I give to the Nokuba—I allow them to go where they want, live how they choose, until I summon them for a mission. But in Mayu's case, that freedom is dangerous."

He paused, his voice growing heavy. "She's in pain. Real pain. And I can already see it turning into rage. That rage will become a desire for revenge, and if she acts on it while she's still grieving, it could get her killed. Father...she's one of mine. A Nokuba. I wasn't there when she needed her leader. If I had made it in time, I could've saved Lord Moya. I could've spared Mayu and Mizo from all this."

Ryoze lowered his head again, his voice breaking slightly. "I don't think I could live with myself if she died because of something I failed to prevent. Please...help me protect her."

Yuuta's eyes softened. He stood and placed a hand on his son's shoulder.

"It's not your fault," Yuuta said. "Every Member of the Nokuba knows that you would lay down your life for them without question."

Ryoze remained silent, still bowing. Yuuta turned to the side and called for one of his messengers.

"Summon Mayu Abahare," he ordered. "Bring her to me."

When Mayu reached the main castle, she was led straight to Master Yuuta's chamber. As the doors opened, she saw Yuuta seated beside Ryoze inside. She walked forward calmly, bowing low before them.

"You called for me, Master Yuuta. I am at your service," she said.

Yuuta nodded. "Mayu, the reason I summoned you is because with your mother's passing, I intend to appoint you as the new Member of the Haras. You've awakened your Reiki, and you are fit for the role."

He paused a moment, then added, "Yes, the plate once protected by your family is now in the hands of the Mutants—but your people still need someone who will make them feel safe. Someone they can rely on. I've already spoken with my son, Lord Ryoze, and he agrees."

Mayu glanced at Ryoze, her expression unreadable. Then she bowed her head again. "As you wish, Master," she said quietly.

After the meeting, she left Yuuta's chamber with Ryoze. As they walked through the hallway in silence, Mayu stopped and turned to him.

"My Lord," she said softly, "please…speak to Master Yuuta. Ask him to reconsider. I want to remain under your command, as a Member of the Nokuba."

Ryoze stopped walking.

He turned his head slightly, his eyes falling on her—but there was no kindness in his expression. His face darkened, his silence carrying more weight than any words. His eyes alone made her feel the answer.

"How dare you question Master Yuuta's decision?"

Mayu's heart sank. She immediately bowed low, her voice trembling.

"I got carried away," she said. "I was out of line…Please forgive me."

Ryoze said nothing. He turned his head and walked away without another word.

Back in the present...

Mayu was still kneeling on the stone path outside the castle, her head bowed to the ground, her body trembling as she cried. Ryoze was already walking away from her, just as he had that day long ago. The past had passed—but the feeling was the same.

She had begged him. Again.

And again, he had walked away.

But what Mayu didn't realize was that Ryoze's rejection had never come from anger or coldness. It came from the one thing he couldn't say out loud—he was trying to protect her.

He knew that if he let her return to the Nokuba, her pain and thirst for revenge would drive her into battles far too dangerous. Battles she might not survive.

Ryoze didn't turn his back because he didn't care. He turned away because he cared too much. Leaving Mayu behind was the only way he knew how to keep her alive.

And now, all she had left was the silence, the ache in her chest, and the name that burned in her mind like fire.

Nobu.

CHAPTER EIGHTEEN
The Mutant and the Mortal

In town, Yasaze crossed paths with Shiro. She greeted him with a warm smile, and for a moment, everything seemed normal.

"How about we go to the lake?" Yasaze suggested, his voice calm. "I could use a bit of quiet...and someone to talk to."

Shiro eagerly agreed, and together they made their way toward the lake. The air was peaceful, the water still under the soft afternoon light. They walked by the edge, the silence between them feeling almost natural at first.

Shiro started talking, trying to make light conversation, but Yasaze stayed unusually quiet. He sat still, facing the water, barely responding.

Shiro grew confused. She glanced at him, wondering why he was acting so distant.

Then, without warning, Yasaze smiled—a calm, knowing smile.

"Were you sent to kill me, Shiro?" he asked, his voice light, almost casual, as he continued staring at the lake.

Shiro stiffened. "What are you talking about?" she asked quickly, her tone slipping.

Yasaze turned his head slowly to face her. His smile didn't fade.

"You don't have to act anymore," he said simply. "I know you're a Mutant, Shiro."

For a brief moment, her expression remained innocent. Then, like a mask dropping, her sweet smile twisted into something darker. The warmth in her eyes disappeared, replaced by cold, cruel malice.

"Is that so?" Shiro said, her voice shifting.

Before Yasaze could move, her body changed, revealing her true form. Shiro—the girl he thought he knew—transformed into Laya, the Fourth Member of the Obake.

In one sudden move, she grabbed Yasaze by the throat, lifting him easily off the ground. Her fingers tightened around his neck.

"I was planning to drag this out a little longer," Laya said, her voice low and mocking. "Maybe get more information out of you. But I guess I'll just kill you now."

Her grip tightened. Yasaze struggled for air as she stared at him coldly, no hint of mercy left in her face.

"Out of curiosity," Laya said, tilting her head as she loosened her grip around Yasaze's throat. "I thought I played the part of your friend perfectly. So tell me—how did you know I was a Mutant?"

Yasaze dropped to his knees, coughing and gasping for air. He steadied himself with one hand on the ground, his body trembling from the sudden attack. After a few shallow breaths, he managed to lift his head.

"Back at the village...when we fought Gazan..." Yasaze rasped. "I saw it. I saw everything."

The memory burned in his mind. He recalled the scene.

When Miji fought to protect the villagers during the battle, Shiro had rushed onto the scene. She had screamed at Gazan, begging him to stop attacking. Miji, desperate to protect her, had shouted back for her to run and hide.

And it looked as if she did. But Yasaze, hidden at a distance, had seen what truly happened.

Instead of running, Shiro had disappeared only for a second—then reappeared behind Miji in a blur. She struck him hard from behind, the attack so fast and brutal that Miji was knocked out instantly.

Gazan stood confused, lowering his guard.

"You pathetic fool..." Shiro said, her voice dropping into something colder, something cruel, as she started to transform into her true nature.

Gazan froze, terror flooding his features.

"Queen Laya...What are you doing here?" he stammered.

"You're ruining my plan, you useless worm," Laya said with a twisted smirk. "I don't forgive mistakes."

"I am sorry, please forgive me...I ask for mercy," Gazan said as he started running away.

Laya didn't even pause. She disappeared from sight for an instant, reappearing right in front of him. With a single, monstrous blow to his face, she struck Gazan down. The force of the attack was so overwhelming that his head exploded instantly.

With her enemy eliminated, Laya struck herself across the side and collapsed onto the ground, faking unconsciousness. By the time the others arrived, they would only see an injured, innocent girl—and no one would suspect the truth.

Only Yasaze, watching silently from the shadows, had seen the truth—and he had kept that secret hidden until now.

Yasaze stared at Shiro with a calmness that was unusual for a man with no powers.

Laya's expression shifted as she listened, genuine confusion flickering across her face.

"I don't get it," she said, narrowing her eyes. "Why did you lie to Tadanaka then? Why didn't you tell anyone what you saw?"

Yasaze, still catching his breath, lifted his head and met her gaze calmly.

"I knew if I told Tadanaka the truth, he would have tried to kill you," he said simply.

For a moment, there was silence. Then Laya burst into a wicked laugh, throwing her head back.

"You make me laugh," she said, stepping closer to him, the grin on her face twisted and cruel. "You really think Tadanaka and his little group could even scratch me? I'm a Member of the Obake, you little shit. Tadanaka and the Gochuu are nothing but roaches crawling under my feet. Do you want me to prove it to you right now?"

Her grin widened cruelly, her Dark Reiki growing heavier around them.

Yasaze didn't flinch. Instead, he smiled.

"True," he said easily. "I know Tadanaka and the Gochuu probably wouldn't stand a chance against you."

Laya's smirk grew, but before she could respond, Yasaze continued.

"But Ryoze and the Nokuba...that's a different story."

At the mention of Ryoze's name, Laya's smile faded. She stayed silent, her eyes narrowing slightly.

After a long moment, she spoke again, her voice lower.

"Then why didn't you tell Ryoze?" she asked.

Yasaze lowered his head slightly, his voice soft when he finally spoke.

"Ever since I was a little boy, I didn't have anyone," he said. "I was always alone. No real friends. No one to really talk to."

He looked up at Laya, his eyes sad but calm.

"Spending time with you...it made me happy. Even if you were just acting, even if everything you said was a lie just to hunt for information, I still treasured it. It still made me feel like I wasn't alone."

There was a pause. His next words came even quieter.

"Even now, knowing that you are a Mutant...I still don't want you to die."

Laya stared at him in disbelief, her mouth slightly open for a moment before she threw her head back and laughed—a sharp, bitter laugh that echoed through the space around them.

"Are you actually stupid?" she said, walking a step closer, her grin wide and wicked. "You don't want me to die? I'm a Mutant, you dumb little runt. I'm the enemy. You're actually funny—pathetic, but funny. Too bad for you...because I'm about to kill you right now."

She raised her hand, her fingers crackling slightly with power.

But Yasaze didn't flinch. Instead, he smiled. A genuine, warm smile.

"I know deep down you feel the same way," he said, his voice steady. "You can pretend all you want, but you can't lie to yourself. You enjoyed it too...even if just a little."

Yasaze smiled softly. He lowered his head slightly, completely calm in the face of death.

"We're all meant to die one day." he said smiling without a trace of fear.

Laya's hand hovered in the air, but she didn't strike. Her fingers trembled slightly, an almost invisible hesitation passing through her.

She had the strength, she had the reason…yet somehow, she couldn't bring herself to land the blow.

The silence stretched between them.

Finally, Laya lowered her hand and scoffed.

"As a matter of fact," she said slowly, her tone dripping with irritation, "it would be a waste to kill you now. I think you'd be more useful to me alive than dead."

Yasaze's smile didn't falter.

"I won't betray my family," he said clearly. "No matter what."

Laya chuckled under her breath, shaking her head.

"Do whatever you want," she said. "I have my own ways of getting what I need."

Yasaze stretched his arms over his head casually, as if the life-or-death tension had never existed.

"Okay then!" he said cheerfully. "Let's go have lunch. I'm starving!"

Laya shot him a glare that could have melted stone.

"Fuck off, you little shit," she snapped. "You really need to understand we're not friends. We were never friends. Don't get the wrong idea."

She took a step past him, brushing his shoulder roughly as she walked away.

"And don't forget," she added darkly, glancing back over her shoulder, "I will kill you sooner or later."

Yasaze chuckled lightly. "Sure you will," he said with a smile as Laya was walking away.

Laya returned to her hidden temple, her footsteps echoing lightly against the stone floor. She thought she was alone until she felt a familiar but unwelcome presence. Jin, the Third Member of the Obake, was already there, leaning casually against one of the pillars as if he had been waiting for her.

His sudden appearance caught her off guard, but she didn't let it show.

"So," Jin said, pushing himself off the wall with a smirk, "Haven't you killed that little useless Toukan yet?"

Laya walked past him without answering immediately, her expression cold and unreadable. She moved deeper into the temple, her footsteps slow and deliberate, before finally turning back to face him.

"Not yet," she said simply. "I'm still getting information out of him."

Jin let out a short laugh, the sound sharp and mocking. "Maybe he really is useless," he said. "Maybe I should just go and kill him myself."

The moment the words left his mouth, Laya's eyes sharpened. She stepped closer, flaring slightly with anger.

"If you dare lay a finger on him," she said, her voice low and dangerous, "I'll rip you apart myself."

Jin raised an eyebrow, clearly amused by her reaction.

"Well, well, well," he said with a mocking grin. "Who would've thought the great Queen of the Mutants, Laya of the Obake, would get attached to a mere human...one who doesn't even have Reiki?"

He chuckled under his breath, but Laya didn't rise to the bait. Her expression remained cold and firm.

"Stop talking nonsense," she said sharply. "Even Lord Shen understands how valuable Yasaze is. The information he holds could change everything for us. He's more useful alive than dead."

She narrowed her eyes at him. "Leave him alone, Jin. I'm warning you."

Jin lifted his hands in mock surrender, the smirk never leaving his face.

"Haha, as you wish, ma'am," he said sarcastically, clearly enjoying himself.

Laya turned away from him without another word, but the tension between them lingered heavy in the air.

CHAPTER NINETEEN
Tracking the Torima

At a small bar tucked away in the village, Mado, Ina, Tadanaka, and Kume sat around a table, sharing a quiet moment away from the pressure of their mission. The mood was light, but not without a trace of unease.

"Mado, you fool," Ina said, setting her drink down with an irritated sigh. "Lord Ryoze sent us on a mission to locate Kanaja, and here we are, sitting in a bar drinking."

Mado leaned back in his chair, his usual easygoing grin on his face.

"Relax, Ina," he said. "You know I've always prioritized Lord Ryoze's orders over everything."

He took a slow sip from his cup before continuing, his tone casual but confident.

"I already sent Harame, Mosha, and the others out to search the area and gather information. They're scouting the streets right now."

He glanced at her, still smiling.

"Don't worry. They know what they're doing. They're bandits, remember? No one's better at sniffing out trouble than them. I'm sure they'll find something useful. So for now, just have a drink and take it easy."

Ina narrowed her eyes at him but didn't argue further. She leaned back in her seat with a huff, clearly still uneasy. Kanaja was the Fifth Member of the Torima, a formidable opponent. For the moment, she let it go.

The door to the bar swung open, drawing the attention of Mado, Ina, Tadanaka, and Kume. Harame and Mosha hurried inside, their footsteps quick and uneven as they made their way toward the table. Harame bowed slightly as he spoke, his tone rushed and serious.

"Lord Mado, we asked around like you ordered. A lot of people here have moved from a small settlement called Somol Village," Harame reported. "They said a Mutant appears there every once in a while, killing humans. Most of the men from that village have turned into bandits and started working under that Mutant."

Mado narrowed his eyes, setting his drink down with a heavy clink. His relaxed attitude vanished immediately as he leaned forward, his voice sharp.

"You idiot," Mado snapped. "I sent you to find solid information, and that's all you can get? This is a mission given to us by Lord Ryoze! You better start taking it seriously!"

Harame flinched but answered quickly, his voice almost defensive.

"You better get serious?! You're the one sitting in a bar drinking alcohol, my Lord," he muttered without thinking.

The words barely left his mouth before Mado shot to his feet, glaring at him with murder in his eyes.

"Do you want to die, fool?" Mado growled, his Reiki rising just enough to make Harame stumble backward in panic.

"I'm sorry, I'm sorry, Lord!" Harame cried, bowing his head repeatedly in apology.

Ina, Tadanaka, and Kume couldn't hold back their laughter. They tried to cover it, but their chuckles filled the table, cutting through the tension for a moment.

Harame, still flustered, remembered something and quickly added, "Lord Mado, there's one more thing. The villagers...they all called that Mutant 'The Kanaja.'"

The moment he said the name, the laughter around the table stopped. Mado, Ina, Tadanaka, and Kume's expressions hardened instantly, the light mood vanishing like it had never been there.

"Kanaja..." Ina repeated under her breath, her voice cold. "That's her."

Mado stood up fully, his face serious, his earlier amusement gone.

"Let's move," he ordered, his voice leaving no room for argument.

"Yes, Lord!" the group answered in unison, pushing back their chairs and rushing out of the bar, their minds focused only on the battle ahead as they made their way toward Somol Village.

The next day, Yasaze and Hala were strolling through the town, the busy streets filled with the usual noise of merchants and villagers. Though Hala spoke to him cheerfully, Yasaze's mind was elsewhere, his thoughts drifting back to Laya and everything that had happened. He walked with his hands loose, distracted, when a familiar voice called out from behind.

"Hey Yasaze, what a pleasant surprise," the voice said warmly.

Yasaze glanced over his shoulder, and there she was—Shiro, standing with a bright smile on her face, looking as harmless and cheerful as ever.

Hala tilted her head curiously and asked, "Who are you?"

With a light laugh, Shiro stepped closer, crouching slightly to meet Hala's gaze. "Hi, sweetheart! My name is Shiro. I'm a friend of Yasaze. What's your name?" she said sweetly.

"My name is Hala. Nice to meet you," Hala replied with a polite smile.

"You're so adorable," Shiro said, gently tapping Hala on the nose with a finger, her voice full of affection.

Yasaze, watching the exchange, gave a small grin and spoke casually. "Care to join us, Shiro? We were just about to have lunch."

For a brief moment, Shiro's eyes shifted. Her gaze, though subtle, turned cold and emotionless as she looked directly at Yasaze. It was only for a heartbeat, but it was enough for him to notice.

Then, just as quickly, she smiled again—bright and innocent, as if nothing had happened. "Sure, I'd love to join you guys," she said happily.

The three of them started walking down the crowded street together, Hala chattering innocently between them. Neither Yasaze nor Hala noticed the shadow watching them from a distance—Jin, hidden in the woods, his sharp gaze locked onto them, silently observing their every move.

Later that afternoon, after parting ways with Yasaze and Hala, Laya returned to her hidden temple. She wasn't expecting company, but as she stepped inside, she found Jin waiting for her again, lounging casually against one of the cold stone pillars.

Laya's eyes narrowed instantly. "Don't worry," Jin said, pushing himself off the pillar lazily. "I'll leave in a second. I just came to tell you something important."

He smiled wickedly, his voice low and deliberate. "You're going to have to kill that Toukan boy."

Laya's expression darkened at once. She stepped closer, her presence sharp and dangerous. "And exactly who do you think you are, daring to command me?" she said, her voice low with rage. "Know your place, Jin."

Jin didn't flinch. He shrugged as if her anger meant nothing. "He serves no purpose anymore," Jin said calmly. "It's time to get rid of him before he becomes a weakness."

Laya's eyes flared with fury, but her voice stayed cold. "Stay out of this, Jin. Last I checked, Yasaze is my concern, not yours."

Jin didn't argue. He stood there watching her in silence, his sharp eyes reading more than she wanted him to.

When she saw he wasn't moving, Laya's voice sliced through the stillness. "Now, if you don't have anything else to say, get lost."

Jin gave her a slow, mocking bow and smiled maliciously. "As you wish," he said before turning and disappearing into the shadows of the temple, leaving Laya alone with her growing frustration.

Mado, Ina, Tadanaka, and Kume walked through Somol Village. The streets were quiet and empty, with no villagers in sight. With many houses looking abandoned, the whole place felt tense and heavy.

They approached a small shop and entered. The old woman standing behind the counter greeted them politely.

"Welcome to my humble shop," she said.

As her eyes quickly studied them, it didn't take her long to realize they were not ordinary travelers. She recognized them immediately as Reiki warriors.

"I'm guessing you have a few questions for me," she said.

Ina stepped forward. "We're sorry for disturbing you at this hour, but we're looking for the Mutant responsible for the problems in this village," she said.

The old woman froze. Her face grew pale, her hands trembling slightly.

"The Kanaja..." she whispered in fear.

"Yes," Ina said. "Kanaja is the one we're after. Please, tell us everything you know."

The old lady nodded and spoke carefully. "Somol Village was once peaceful. Everything changed when the Kanaja arrived. It terrorized the people and brought ruin. Many Reiki warriors answered our call for help, but none of them returned. Not a single trace was found. Now, Kanaja controls the village. Many men here have joined her. Every night, people disappear."

"Thank you," Mado said casually. "Don't worry. We'll handle it."

As they stepped outside, Ina turned serious. "Mado, you and Tadanaka take the north side of the village. Kume and I will cover the south. If any of you encounter Kanaja, release your Reiki fully so we can sense it and rush to help. Do the same if you sense ours."

Mado nodded, his usual grin appearing. He clapped Tadanaka lightly on the back. "Sounds good. Let's move, kid," he said as the two headed toward the north side, while Ina and Kume moved toward the south.

CHAPTER TWENTY
Held at the Edge

In the main village, Yasaze was wandering through the streets, spending his afternoon helping elderly villagers carry supplies and run errands. He had managed to slip away from his assigned bodyguards as usual, preferring the freedom of the village over the constant watch of escorts.

Laya watched him silently from a distance, keeping herself hidden among the crowds. She followed him carefully, her light, precise steps concealing her presence. She stayed close as Yasaze finished helping the villagers and eventually made his way toward the woods, heading back toward his home.

Laya continued tailing him through the trees, her mind darkening with every step.

"I should end this now," she muttered under her breath, eyes locked onto Yasaze's back. "I have to kill him while I still have the chance."

She prepared herself, focusing her strength, waiting for the right moment to strike. Her gaze sharpened, her muscles tensed. She was moments away from launching her attack—

But then she noticed something.

Another Mutant, hidden in the shadows, was watching Yasaze with clear intent to kill. Without thinking, Laya moved. Her body reacted before her mind could catch up. In a blur of motion, she closed the distance and struck the Mutant down, killing him instantly before he could move on Yasaze.

She stood over the body for a moment, stunned by her own actions.

"What am I doing…?" she whispered to herself in shock. "Why did I protect Yasaze?"

Up ahead, Yasaze had heard the noise and turned back curiously. His eyes searched the trees until he spotted a figure walking toward him. Recognizing her immediately, he waved cheerfully.

"Shir—I mean, Laya! What are you doing here?" Yasaze called out, clearly excited to see her.

Laya crossed her arms, looking unimpressed as she approached.

"I'm pretty sure that empty head of yours doesn't have a brain inside," she said sharply. "Don't you ever pay attention to your surroundings?"

Yasaze just smiled at her, trying to figure out what she meant but not really understanding.

"Don't even bother trying to understand," she said, rolling her eyes. "Your brain's clearly on vacation."

Yasaze chuckled and shrugged it off without taking offense.

"I was just about to head home," he said casually. "But since you're here, how about we go chill by the lake?"

Laya narrowed her eyes at him.

"What part of 'We aren't friends' don't you understand?" she snapped.

"Come on, please! Just for a little while," Yasaze said with a wide grin. "Please, please, please, please—"

"Fine, fine!" Laya interrupted, holding up her hand to shut him up. "Just do me a favor and stop talking."

They sat together by the lake, the surface of the water still and quiet. Yasaze spoke freely, chatting and laughing, his voice light with happiness. As he talked, Laya—still in her human form—watched him closely. For a moment, she caught herself smiling without meaning to. Seeing the genuine happiness in Yasaze's eyes stirred something unfamiliar inside her.

"Are you okay, Laya? Why are you smiling?" Yasaze asked suddenly, tilting his head with curiosity.

Realizing what she was doing, Laya immediately wiped the smile from her face and snapped back to her usual cold demeanor. "Who's smiling?" she said sharply. "It's one thing to be an idiot, but being a blind idiot puts you on an entirely new level."

Yasaze laughed without a care in the world. "Hahaha, sure," he said, grinning widely.

Laya was about to yell at him again, but then something shifted in the air. Her entire body tensed as a heavy, dark presence washed over her senses. Her playful irritation vanished, replaced by serious alarm. She turned her head sharply, scanning the woods behind them.

"Please tell me this isn't happening," she muttered to herself, her heart pounding as she spotted a figure lurking in the shadows. Jin stood half-hidden among the trees, his cold eyes locked directly onto Yasaze.

Panic raced through Laya's mind. *"Shit...shit...this is bad, very bad,"* she thought desperately. "What do I do?"

Noticing the sudden change in her expression, Yasaze leaned closer. "Is everything okay, Laya?" he asked innocently.

Without taking her eyes off the threat, Laya spoke in a low, serious tone. "Listen carefully, kid. When I give the signal—run. No questions, no turning around. Just run."

Yasaze blinked, confused by the sudden shift in her voice, but nodded hesitantly.

Laya clenched her fists, preparing herself. *"I guess I'll have to fight him here,"* she thought grimly.

As Jin prepared to strike and Laya tensed, ready to transform into her Mutant form, both of them suddenly froze. An overwhelming wave of monstrous power rolled through the air. Laya and Jin turned their heads at the same time, their faces pale with shock.

Out from the trees, calmly and steadily, walked Ryoze. His presence alone was enough to make the air feel heavier with every step.

As Jin's eyes narrowed, he momentarily weighed his options. "I don't think I'm ready to fight him...not yet," he thought grimly. Without another word, Jin disappeared into the woods, vanishing before Ryoze could spot him.

"Big brother Ryoze!" Yasaze cried happily, running to him and throwing his arms around his brother.

Ryoze smiled warmly, placing a hand on Yasaze's head. "Hey, dear Yasaze. I didn't expect to find you here," he said gently.

Yasaze turned back to where Laya stood, waving at her over excitedly. "Shiro, I want to introduce you to my elder brother—Ryoze!" he said proudly.

Laya stepped forward, bowing her head low, careful to hide the tension she felt.

She already knew who Ryoze was, but she played her part perfectly.

"Ryoze…Lord Ryoze Toukan?" she said, her voice full of feigned surprise. "Please forgive me, my Lord. I didn't realize it was you."

Giving a kind smile, Ryoze shook his head. "Please, raise your head. There's no need to be so formal. Any friend of Yasaze's is a friend of mine," he said warmly.

Looking down at Yasaze with a fond smile, Ryoze continued. "Naru is cooking tonight, and Hala has been asking about you nonstop. Will you come home with me for dinner?"

Yasaze's face lit up immediately. "Of course! I'm actually getting hungry," he said excitedly, then turned quickly toward Laya. "Can Shiro come too?"

Laya blinked, caught off guard by the invitation.

"Absolutely," Ryoze said. "She's more than welcome."

"You honor me, Lord Ryoze. I truly appreciate the offer," Laya said politely, trying to regain her composure. "But I have to return home. There are chores waiting for me."

Ryoze's smile didn't fade. "Your chores can wait. You are the first person Yasaze has ever introduced to me as a friend. It would be rude of me not to invite you properly. Please, I insist," he said.

Laya hesitated. Part of her told her to refuse again, but another part of her thought differently. "If I go with them," she reasoned silently, "I might actually get valuable information."

Finally, she bowed her head once more. "You honor me, my Lord. I humbly accept your invitation," she said smoothly.

Smiling, Ryoze placed a gentle hand on Yasaze's shoulder. Together, the three of them started walking back toward Ryoze's castle.

CHAPTER TWENTY-ONE
Mutant Among the Toukan

A while later, the three of them arrived at Ryoze's castle. As soon as they stepped inside, a small voice cried out with excitement.

"Uncle Yasaze!" Hala shouted as she ran toward him, throwing herself into Yasaze's arms. He caught her easily and laughed, spinning her once before hugging her tightly.

"What a pleasant surprise," Naru said as she approached, wiping her hands on a cloth as she finished setting the table.

"Big sister Naru, it's nice to see you," Yasaze said with a wide grin. "I want you to meet my friend, Shiro."

Naru greeted Laya politely. The rest of the household welcomed her warmly soon after, completely unaware of her true nature. Laya sat with them at the dinner table, forcing herself to remain composed. She hated how much she was enjoying their company, how easy it was to fall into the rhythm of laughter and light conversation.

After the meal, Yasaze and Hala played together near the porch, their laughter filling the air. Laya helped Naru clear the dishes, moving carefully, every action controlled. From his seat on the porch, Ryoze watched quietly through the open sliding door, his thoughtful gaze fixed on Laya.

"Shiro," Ryoze called, his voice even and polite. "Would you sit with me for a moment? I would like to speak with you briefly, if you don't mind."

"Of course, my Lord," Laya said, bowing her head slightly.

As she walked toward him, her mind raced. She forced herself to stay calm, reminding herself that he didn't know the truth. *"Stay normal,"* she thought. *"Don't give him a reason to doubt you."*

She sat down beside him, keeping a respectful distance. The moment her eyes met his, she understood she would need to choose her words carefully. She wasn't speaking to an ordinary man; she was sitting next to the leader of the Nokuba—a man known not just for strength, but for intelligence and ruthlessness.

At this point, Laya no longer cared about gaining information. She only wanted to survive the night without exposing herself.

"Shiro," Ryoze began, his voice low and reflective. "Ever since Yasaze was born, I have always felt a deep pity for him. He is the only human ever born without Reiki. I have seen him try countless times to grow stronger, only to fail. I have watched him struggle to find his place, surrounded by a family of warriors, born from a line of strength. He is the son of Yuuta Toukan, the strongest Reiki warrior alive, and yet he alone carries nothing. I can't imagine the pain he feels, standing among us."

Ryoze paused for a moment, glancing at Yasaze laughing in the distance with Hala.

"There are times it is difficult even for me to look him in the eyes. My sister Shita and I once made a vow to our mother on her deathbed, swearing that we would protect Yasaze no matter what. That vow has never left me. I would gladly give my life for him," Ryoze said, his voice steady. "But...how do I protect him from the pain inside himself?"

He smiled softly, a rare expression from a man of his stature.

"Yet something has changed. I have always seen Yasaze smiling, but now I can tell he is truly happy for the first time. And I believe," Ryoze continued as he turned his gaze back to Laya, "you are a large part of that change."

Laya followed his eyes to Yasaze and Hala. Without realizing it, she smiled too.

"I can see it clearly," Ryoze said. "Your presence means more to him than you realize. And I thank you for that."

Without warning, Ryoze bowed his head in gratitude.

Laya froze, completely stunned. A man as powerful and respected as Ryoze Toukan, bowing humbly to her—a lie, a Mutant hiding among his family.

"My Lord! Please, I beg you, rise!" Laya said quickly, her voice shaken. "I am not worthy of such honor. Your gratitude is already more than enough."

Ryoze lifted his head, smiling warmly. "It would mean a great deal to me if you continued to bring joy into his life, Shiro," he said.

"Of course, my Lord," Laya replied, bowing deeply. "You have my word."

Yasaze ran toward them, grinning.

"What are you two talking about?" he asked as he sat down beside them.

"I was just getting to know your friend a little better," Ryoze said, gently patting his little brother's head.

"She's wonderful, don't you think?" Yasaze said proudly.

"Yes," Ryoze replied, smiling at Laya. "She most certainly is."

Quickly excusing herself, Laya returned to help Naru with the cleanup.

"So, what is your profession, Shiro?" Naru asked casually as they worked side by side.

"I'm a tailor," Laya answered quickly. "I work from my home. People bring their clothes to me for repairs and adjustments."

"A tailor, huh? Is that so?" Naru said, watching her carefully.

Laya remained calm, but inside her mind raced. *"Naru Akaryu... Second Member of the Nokuba. They say she's as terrifying as she is powerful,"* she thought.

"Have you ever trained?" Naru asked, her tone light but her eyes sharp. "Tried to develop your Reiki?"

"No," Laya said smoothly. "I've always hated violence. Since I was young, I have avoided it. I wanted to live a quiet life, far from bloodshed and conflict."

Naru smiled faintly, but it did not reach her eyes.

"Oh really?" Naru said. "Because your eyes...they tell a different story. You have the eyes of a killer."

Laya forced a light laugh. "Well, maybe that's a good thing," she said. "One look at me, and criminals think twice before trying anything."

"Yeah...a good thing," Naru said, her smile cold and her stare sharp.

A heavy silence fell between them. Laya felt every second stretch, her muscles tense and ready to react. She was prepared for a sudden attack if it came, her mind racing with possibilities.

Hala's voice called out from the next room. Blinking once, Naru calmly turned toward her daughter.

She excused herself and left the room without another word, leaving Laya standing there, tension slowly draining from her body.

After that tense encounter, Laya approached Ryoze and Yasaze. She bowed respectfully.

"Lord Ryoze," she said. "Thank you for graciously inviting me to share a meal with your family. It was truly an honor. With your permission, I will now take your leave."

Ryoze stood and smiled. "There's no need for such formality. I meant what I said. Any friend of Yasaze is family here. If you ever need anything, don't hesitate to ask. Take care, and I hope we meet again soon."

"I will see you soon, Yasaze," Laya said with a smile before making her way toward the castle gates.

Passing through the quiet woods cautiously, she made sure she wasn't being followed before eventually arriving back at her temple. As she crossed the threshold, her form shifted back into her true Mutant body. The tension she had been carrying all night finally left her in a slow, shaky breath.

Suddenly, a voice spoke from the shadows, cold and familiar.

"Welcome back, Laya," it said.

She froze and turned sharply. From beyond the stone pillars, Shen emerged, stepping forward with the same overwhelming presence he always carried. Laya bowed immediately.

"Forgive me, Shen," she said quietly. "I didn't realize you were here."

"I hope you'll excuse the intrusion," Shen said calmly. "But something told me I should be here tonight."

He stepped closer, the usual chill in his voice sharpening.

"The Reiki warriors are preparing for an all-out assault," Shen said. "Until now, they only defended, killing Mutants when necessary. They only sought to maintain peace and protect the plates. With the Mutotsu's rebirth nearing, their strategy has changed. They are attacking first, trying to weaken us before the real battle begins."

He gave a cold laugh.

"They believe thinning our numbers will give them a better chance at surviving the Mutotsu's awakening. Fools. They have no idea what they are facing."

He stepped closer, his voice lowering.

"Still, don't let your guard down. Especially when facing the Haras or the Nokuba. They are not to be underestimated. Seken and Gerad made that mistake—and it cost them their lives."

"I understand," Laya said. "I will carry your warning with me."

Shen studied her silently for a moment, sensing the tension still clinging to her.

"You've just returned," he said calmly. "Where were you?"

Laya lowered her head slightly before answering. "I was at Ryoze Toukan's castle with Yasaze," she said. "Ryoze appeared and, without giving me much of a choice, invited me to dinner. Refusing would have drawn suspicion."

Shen's expression sharpened instantly. "Ryoze's castle?" he repeated, his tone growing colder. "What happened?"

"I played my part," Laya replied steadily. "I didn't get any valuable information, but my cover stayed intact. None of them suspected who I really am."

Shen nodded thoughtfully.

"And your impression of Ryoze?" he asked.

Laya's voice grew quieter.

"I have never met a human like him," she said. "He didn't release his Reiki, but standing near him was suffocating. He moved calmly and spoke softly, but his presence was crushing. It felt like standing before a sleeping predator—one wrong move, and you wouldn't survive. And Naru...she was different. Cold, sharp, immediate. She watched everything, missing nothing. Where Ryoze was a silent threat, Naru was the blade already drawn. Together...they are terrifying."

Shen smiled darkly.

"Like father, like son," he said. "I fought Ryoze once, back when he awakened his Reiki. He carries the same monstrous pressure Yuuta does. They hide it behind kindness, behind humility, but make no mistake—underneath, they are monsters."

Shen's eyes gleamed with excitement as he spoke the final words.

"This will be fun. Killing Ryoze will be a pleasure."

CHAPTER TWENTY-TWO
Toast and Tension

Back in Somol Village, Ina and Kume were exactly where they were supposed to be—positioned on the south side, alert, focused, and ready for anything. Their movements were quiet and purposeful, every step calculated as they patrolled the darkened streets. The villagers were afraid to come out, and for good reason. They knew what Kanaja was capable of. Ina and Kume did not relax. They remained sharp, prepared for the possibility that Kanaja might show at any moment.

On the other side of the village, things were a little less organized. Mado and Tadanaka were technically in the north...but if anyone considered the village bar to be a legitimate tactical outpost, maybe they could claim to be in position.

Tadanaka sat stiffly across from Mado, visibly uncomfortable, shifting in his seat every few seconds as if that alone might make the situation feel more appropriate. The bar was dim, quiet, and poorly maintained. A few locals sat in the corners drinking in silence. Mado, however, seemed perfectly at home, sipping from his full glass without a care in the world.

"Lord Mado," Tadanaka said, lowering his voice in an effort to avoid attention. "We really shouldn't be here right now. This isn't part of the plan. Kanaja could show up any moment, and we're supposed to be outside patrolling the northern side—not sitting around in a bar drinking. If something happens while we're here, people could get hurt. We need to stick to the plan and stay sharp. Let's go before it's too late."

Mado didn't even look up. He took another slow sip, sighed in satisfaction, then finally set his cup down on the table with exaggerated patience.

"For the love of all things sacred, would you please shut up?" he said calmly. "Just zip it. Honestly. Last time I checked, I was the one in charge." He finally looked up, locking eyes with Tadanaka. "You're starting to sound like my nagging wife—which is impressive, considering I don't even have one."

Tadanaka blinked, unsure if he was supposed to laugh or be offended.

"Look, kid," Mado continued, pointing a finger lazily at him, "I don't dislike you. You've got spirit. Annoying, overly talkative spirit, but it's something. However, let's get one thing straight. I only take orders from one man—your brother, Ryoze. That man has earned my loyalty a hundred times over. I'd follow him into hell and back without question. But you?" Mado leaned back with a smirk. "You're not Ryoze. So unless he shows up right now and tells me to stop drinking, I'm not moving. Not an inch."

Tadanaka opened his mouth to argue again, but Mado raised his hand to stop him.

"In fact, do yourself a favor. Sit your uptight self down, pick up that glass, and have a drink with me. Make a toast to something. Your youth, your noble cause, your tragic sense of duty—whatever works for you. It's tradition. You can't say no to your superior, especially not one who could toss you across this bar without spilling his drink. And if you still refuse," he said with a grin, "then I'll have to kill you. Politely, of course. Respectfully. Maybe even with a toast."

Tadanaka let out a long sigh and stared at the untouched glass in front of him. He clearly didn't want to give in, but there wasn't much choice. Finally, he picked it up and took a reluctant sip.

The moment the drink touched his lips, Mado lit up. He slammed a hand on the table and burst out laughing. With one massive clap on Tadanaka's back—strong enough to knock the wind out of him—Mado leaned in, grinning like they had just sealed a pact.

"There it is!" Mado shouted. "Now that's the spirit! Look at you, finally starting to act like a real warrior. We drink, we fight, we live!"

Tadanaka rubbed his back where Mado had smacked him, muttering something under his breath. He already regretted the decision—but deep down, he knew there was no changing Mado. All he could do now was hope Kanaja didn't show up while they were mid-toast.

On the southern edge of the village, under the night's quiet hum, Kume sat cross-legged against a stone, slowly running a rough rock along the edge of her blade. The gentle scrape of metal echoed softly in silence. She paused for a moment and glanced sideways, curious about what Ina was up to.

Her eyes landed on Ina seated a few feet away, perfectly composed. She sat in a formal position, legs neatly folded beneath her, back straight as a rod, hands resting calmly on her lap. Her sword lay at her side untouched, her eyes remaining closed in silent meditation. There was a stillness about her, a focused peace that Kume did not quite understand, but admired.

As Kume's gaze drifted, something caught her eye—the ring on Ina's finger. It glimmered faintly in the moonlight, delicate yet commanding, carved with decorative lettering. She looked closely, reading the word engraved on it: Nokuba.

Kume found herself staring without realizing it, drawn to the ring's beauty and the mystery it carried.

"You like it?" A soft voice broke the silence.

Kume jumped slightly as Ina opened her eyes, her voice calm and steady, almost as if she had sensed Kume's curiosity all along.

"Yes....It is beautiful," Kume said honestly, eyes still fixed on the ring.

"Thank you," Ina replied with a gentle nod. "It is given to all the Nokuba Members. Lord Ryoze himself gifted it to us when we were chosen by him as Members of the Nokuba," Ina said.

Kume blinked, clearly impressed. The weight of the title Nokuba settled into her mind. She opened her mouth, ready to ask something, but stopped herself. The question felt too personal, too forward. She glanced away awkwardly, unsure if it was her place.

"It's okay," Ina said suddenly, her voice warm and knowing. She offered a small, encouraging smile. "Ask me."

Kume hesitated only for a second before giving in to her curiosity. "How...how did you become one of the Nokuba?"

Ina smiled for a moment. "The Nokuba, huh..." she said softly, as she tilted her head back, eyes tracing the stars above them. For a moment, she didn't speak.

Kume stayed quiet, sensing that whatever Ina was about to say was not something she shared often.

As Ina's eyes slowly returned to hers, she gave a small, thoughtful nod. "Alright," she said softly. "I will tell you."

She shifted slightly, her tone growing calm and steady. "It was about six years ago...when everything started to change for me," she began, eyes distant as the past came to life in her mind.

Ina was born into one of the four great Royal families, Laitonn, the clan of lightning. As tradition dictated, the women of the Royal bloodlines possessed remarkable energy and Reiki, but were rarely expected to become warriors. And within the Laitonn Clan, that expectation was even stricter. Strength in spirit was respected. Strength in battle, though? That was left to the men.

But Ina had never been like the others. She grew alongside her two closest friends, Naru and Mayu, daughters of high status just like her, but different in every way. Naru and Mayu were sharp, driven, and unyielding. Every morning they trained, perfecting their control over their Reiki, pushing their bodies beyond their limits. Ina, by contrast, had always been gentle, soft-spoken, kind, calm. But deep within, she held a quiet determination that burned just as bright.

As the years passed, Naru eventually married Lord Ryoze, famed leader of the Nokuba, the most elite force in the land. After their marriage, Naru and Mayu both earned their place among the Nokuba. It was a huge accomplishment. The Nokuba weren't just strong, they were the best of the best, feared across all of Alard and respected by everyone. And the power to choose them belonged solely to Ryoze himself. Not even his father, Master Yuuta, the ruler of the lands, could dictate who joined his ranks.

Ina admired her friends. But more than that, she wanted to prove she could stand among them. She dreamed of becoming the first female warrior in the history of her clan, a legacy built on lightning, pride and silence.

Many of the clan's elders scoffed at her training. To them, it was a waste of time. A girl like Ina was meant to be a figure of grace, not a warrior. But they could not stop her, not when her father, Baraqu Laitonn, was the head of the Laitonn Clan and one of the Four Members of the Haras. Baraqu was one of the most powerful warriors alive, and the elders, despite disagreeing, did not dare act against his will.

One evening, sensing her frustration, Baraqu approached her as she was finishing her training. His voice was calm but resolute.

"Don't pay attention to what they say," he told her. "You can be anything you choose to be. You're my daughter, and if any of those wrinkled old fools so much as look at you funny...I will personally send them to their grave."

He burst into hearty laughter, and Ina laughed with him, the tension in her chest finally easing.

Then came the day Lord Ryoze paid their castle a visit. It wasn't unexpected, after all, her father was one of the Haras Members, but for Ina, something was different. She had met Ryoze before, briefly, but this time...she felt it.

His presence.

Even standing still, Ryoze radiated power. It wasn't just strength; it was control, leadership and Reiki so dense it almost made the air hum around him. As Ina stood watching him from afar, something within her shifted.

She wanted to serve under him. She wanted to be one of them, a Nokuba. One of the warriors Ryoze himself trusted to carry out missions that shaped the land.

She stepped forward, bowed to Ryoze, and said something she had never said to anyone before.

"I know I am not ready...but one day, you'll choose me as a Member of the Nokuba."

Ryoze looked at her for a moment, a small smile forming at the corner of his mouth. Her father, standing beside him, said nothing, but his expression was proud.

"Alright then," Ryoze said. "Train hard. And don't forget those words."

From that day forward, Ina trained harder than ever. Day and night, through pain and exhaustion, through torn muscles and broken bones. Her Royal blood gave her faster healing, but it did not erase the agony. Still, she never stopped. Every injury, every bruise was a step closer to her goal.

Eventually, she arrived at Ryoze's castle. It had been a while. She was clearly stronger. Her Reiki was sharper, more refined. She was no longer the gentle girl watching from afar.

Naru greeted her at the gates with a warm smile, but Ina did not come for pleasantries.

"I am here to see Lord Ryoze," she said.

When Ryoze finally stepped out, she met his gaze without flinching.

"I'm ready," she said. "Fight me."

Ryoze looked at her in silence for a long moment, then smiled faintly.

"Are you sure?"

"Yes," she replied.

Ryoze stepped forward, releasing half of his Reiki.

That was all it took.

The air shifted.

The moment he unleashed even half of his Reiki, a powerful gust erupted around him without warning, as if the wind had been sleeping until he summoned it. It wasn't just air moving, it was force, it was presence, it was a storm given form. The sky seemed to respond, clouds shifting unnaturally above them.

Ina's heart pounded in her chest. Her feet slid slightly as the wind shoved against her body from all directions, pressing against her skin, wrapping around her like a force testing her resolve.

Her legs trembled. Her arms locked. Her instincts screamed that she was standing at the center of a hurricane.

She had never felt anything like it. His Reiki didn't feel like energy. It felt like judgement.

"So this is what true power feels like..." she thought, frozen in place. "What did he go through to become this strong? How much pain? How much discipline?"

Ryoze's voice cut through the wind.

"Don't freeze. Attack."

His words snapped her back into herself.

Ina attacked, flaring. Flickering bolts of lightning danced along her arms as she channeled all the Reiki she could muster.

She struck fast. Her blade arced with a thread of electricity, every swing charged with intent. As her foot hit the ground, a thin crackle of lighting snapped at her heels.

But Ryoze didn't falter.

The wind around him responded, rising like a living barrier. Each of Ina's electrified strikes was met with an elegant deflection, sometimes with a tilt of his blade, other times with nothing but a subtle shift of his stance. The wind bent her lightning off course, diffused it, scattered it like sparks in a storm.

Still Ina pushed forward, ignoring the burning in her limbs. Another swing, this one with a small surge of lightning behind it, crackled dangerously close to Ryoze's shoulder.

He moved like mist in a hurricane. Untouched.

Then he struck.

With a simple wave of his hand and a burst of wind-infused Reiki, he knocked her off balance. A pressure-filled gust struck her in the chest, sending her flying backward. She hit the ground hard, her sword spinning away.

Dust swirled around her as she gasped for breath.

Ryoze still hadn't broken a sweat.

He walked forward, slow and composed, his Reiki gently fading, the winds calming around him as if dismissed.

"Go home; you need to train harder."

Ina tried to speak, but the words wouldn't come. Her chest ached, as did her pride.

"He is on another level entirely...I couldn't touch him. Not once," she thought, lowering her head in defeat as Ryoze walked away.

Then...clink.

She opened her eyes.

A ring had landed before her, resting gently in the dirt.

Her hands trembled as she reached for it. The moment she touched it, she knew. Its weight was heavier than any sword she had ever held.

She look up, stunned. Already turning, Ryoze paused, glancing over his shoulder with the faintest smile.

"Come back tomorrow, and I will give you your first mission as a Nokuba," Ryoze said.

She froze, trying as hard as she could to hold back her tears. Her chest ached, not from exhaustion, but from the weight of everything she had carried for years. The whispers from the elders. The persistent doubt. The constant cold glances that said she didn't belong, just because she was born into a role she dared to challenge.

She had been chosen.

She bowed in gratitude, both knees pressing to the ground along with her forehead.

"You believed in me...when even my own people wouldn't. And for that, I owe you everything. I will never take this for granted. I will carry your name, your command, and this ring with pride, until the day I fall," Ina said.

Ryoze took a step toward her, his tone firm but warm.

"Then rise, Ina."

She looked up slowly, sill trembling.

"From this moment on, you are a Nokuba. You carry my name, my command... and my protection."

He paused, just long enough for the words to sink in.

"And as long as you wear that ring, no one will ever question your place again."

That was the moment it all broke inside her—the fear, the doubt, the memories of every dismissive whisper saying she couldn't.

She wept. Not from weakness, but from the overwhelming weight of being seen...and accepted.

Naru stood to the side in quiet stillness, her eyes misted, her smile full of pride. One tear slid down her cheek, and she let it fall.

She had always believed in Ina.

Now Ryoze did too.

The memory faded, not with silence, but with peace.

CHAPTER TWENTY-THREE
What We Aim to Become

Ina opened her eyes slowly, the soft hum of night returning around her. Her voice was calm now, her expression serene.

Kume sat across from her, wide-eyed and silent. She had barely blinked.

"That's...incredible," she whispered.

Ina gave a faint smile, her hand resting over the ring on her finger. "It was the moment everything changed. The day I stopped chasing approval...and found my place," Ina said, smiling.

They shared a quiet smile, an unspoken sense of peace hanging between them after their conversation.

But it didn't last long.

Suddenly, Ina's expression shifted. Her body tensed, eyes narrowing as she turned her head sharply toward the north.

She felt it. A surge of Reiki—sharp, desperate, and chaotic.

"Tadanaka...he's fighting," she whispered, her tone dropping.

Her hand moved instinctively to the hilt of her sword, already on her feet.

"They've encountered Kanaja," she muttered to herself, then looked over to Kume. "Let's go! They found Kanaja!" she shouted as she dashed into the village, her Reiki flaring faintly with urgency.

Kume jumped up immediately, snapping to attention.

"Yes, Lord Ina!" she called, rapidly following Ina into the village.

A few minutes earlier—North side of the village...

The dimly lit bar reeked of cheap liquor. Mado was slouched over the table, passed out, a half-finished bottle still in his hand. He had clearly overdone it—again.

Tadanaka, sitting across from him, had only drunk a few sips. His posture was upright, eyes unfocused but alert, when a piercing scream echoed from outside the bar.

Tadanaka stood immediately, nudging Mado with the back of his hand. "Did you hear that?" Tadanaka asked.

Mado groaned, shifting his head against the table.

"Piss off...go play hero, I'm sleepy," Mado mumbled.

Tadanaka didn't wait. He turned and pushed through the door, stepping out into the village. The scream had come from just down the street.

He followed the sound quickly. As he rounded the corner, he saw it—a man on the ground, crawling backward, eyes wide in terror as something loomed over him.

Kanaja.

KANAJA

Tadanaka acted immediately. He rushed forward, drawing his blade and unleashing his Reiki.

He stepped between Kanaja and the man just in time to block the first strike. "Run!" he shouted over his shoulder.

The man didn't argue. He took off into the village, disappearing into the dark.

Kanaja tilted her head, a sinister smile spreading across her face.

"More Reiki warriors. Haven't I killed enough of you already?" she said mockingly.

Tadanaka swallowed hard. He could already feel it—the pressure, the imbalance of power. Kanaja—the Fifth Member of the Torima. He felt it. She was stronger, faster.

But he had no choice.

Narrowing his stance, he summoned every ounce of his Reiki. Though faint, his wind rose in response, twisting at his arms and swirling at his feet.

He charged.

Tadanaka struck with speed, using light, agile movements, cutting from all angles. His wind danced with each attack—guiding, sharpening—but not enough. Not nearly.

Kanaja blocked every attack with terrifying ease, barely shifting its weight.

"You're trying, I'll give you that."

Then she moved.

In a blink, she lashed out. Tadanaka blocked just in time, but the impact jarred his arms, nearly knocking the blade from his hand.

"Shit...this is bad," Tadanaka grunted, staggering back.

Kanaja laughed darkly. "Is that it? Try to block this." She surged forward, this time with real intent.

Tadanaka exhaled sharply and closed his eyes. He planted his feet, pulled everything he had into his center, and drew the wind in around him—not commanding it, but holding it close.

He opened his eyes just as Kanaja's strike came down.

He met her strike with his blade—and wind.

The force of impact cracked the ground beneath him, dust and energy exploding outward. He staggered, but didn't fall.

Kanaja paused, "Well...I did not expect that from you," she said, mildly surprised.

Tadanaka's breath was ragged. *"One hit and I'm already struggling... If she keeps this up, I won't last much longer,"* he thought.

Then came the sound of slow, amused clapping behind him. Tadanaka looked over his shoulder to find Mado.

He strolled casually into view like he had just rolled out of bed, wearing only one slipper and his ripped clothes. His hair was a mess. His eyes were half-lidded. He was holding a plate of dumplings in one hand, munching on one like this was just a late-night snack break.

"Well damn, didn't know you had it in you, kid. I was going to kill both of you for being loud and waking me up...but this? This is actually entertaining," Mado said, speaking around a mouthful of food.

Before Tadanaka could respond, two figures sprinted into view—Ina and Kume, their arrival sending a subtle but powerful shift through the atmosphere.

Ina's eyes narrowed immediately, sensing the Dark Reiki coming off Kanaja.

Mado glanced over his shoulder, still chewing.

"Oh good, Ina! Perfect timing. Come watch—Tadanaka was just about to get his ass kicked. I brought snacks," Mado said, waving a dumpling in the air.

Kanaja, fully annoyed, decided to resume her onslaught against Tadanaka. Another flurry of strikes crashed into him like a storm. He blocked them— barely—but each impact was shaking his whole body.

"Hey, Gochuu girl, so you are just going to stand there and watch your leader get bullied? Come on, have some dignity," Mado added lazily, not even looking at her.

"Yes, Lord Mado!" Kume said without hesitation. She surged forward, blade drawn, and drove into the fight beside Tadanaka.

Together, they began to push back—not evenly, but effectively. Kume's strikes were fast and clean, balancing Tadanaka's defensive rhythm. They covered for each other. Their teamwork was admirable.

Ina's gaze was locked on Kanaja, eyes already reading the Dark Reiki pattern swirling around her body. Ina stepped forward, ready to join them—but Mado extended his arm, blocking her path.

He was not smiling anymore. His eyes, often half-lidded with amusement, were now cold and focused.

"No, let them fight," he said quietly.

Ina did not argue but looked at him for a moment, then nodded silently and stepped back.

Mado then started laughing again, giving them a mock cheer from the sidelines. "Not bad, you two! And hey—don't stress. Worst-case scenario: you die," he said, laughing.

Kume nearly tripped. "He always talks like that?" she asked, shocked. "Just focus," Tadanaka replied.

The battle raged on.

Tadanaka and Kume worked like one body. Tadanaka's Wind Reiki supported Kume's attacks, her precision gave him openings to breathe. For a moment, it seemed like they could hold their ground. Maybe even outlast it.

Kanaja was now visibly irritated by their resilience. Her body began to darken, and her Reiki darkened visibly. Black energy cracking through her skin like veins of ink. The air grew cold, the ground beneath them trembled.

And from the sidelines—Mado stopped smiling.

He stood straighter. His eyes sharpened.

"Shit...," he muttered, dropping his dumpling. His playful expression fell away completely. Now he looked...dangerous.

Kanaja moved faster than either Tadanaka or Kume could react. Her claws glowed with pure, condensed malice. She struck with the force of a killing blow, aiming to end them both in a single strike.

Tadanaka and Kume tried to brace. They knew—if this landed, they were done.

The attack hit.

But instead of pain...there was silence.

Dust exploded across the village. As the smoke cleared, Tadanaka opened one eye. Kume gasped softly.

There, standing in front of them—calm, unshaken—was Mado.

He stood with one hand raised, having caught Kanaja's full-force attack with a single palm. The street cracked beneath his feet, and the Reiki around him pulsed—not aggressive, but immovable.

"Hey now...that was a little harsh, don't you think?" Mado said, staring at Kanaja with a hard expression.

Tadanaka and Kume were stunned into silence.

He hadn't even drawn his sword. Mado pushed Kanaja's arm away with ease and rolled his shoulders.

"Alright, guess nap time's over." Mado sighed. He stepped forward. "Move aside, kids. Let me show you how it's done."

They obeyed instinctively, stepping back as Mado walked forward, every movement smooth, deliberate.

"Let's play a game. You've got three minutes. Do whatever you want—go all out. I won't block. I won't attack. If you land a hit even once, you win," Mado said, as he raised three fingers.

He tilted his head slightly, smirking again. "But if the timer runs out...it's my turn." He cracked his neck.

Tadanaka and Kume stood frozen behind him, wide-eyed.

"Is he serious?" Kume whispered. "No idea...but I think Kanaja should be worried," Tadanaka muttered.

Fueled with rage, Kanaja charged. She unleashed everything—wild strikes, Reiki blasts, rapid movements.

Mado didn't move.

He dodged every attack with lazy, fluid steps—barely even trying. Kanaja's claws scraped empty air. Her Reiki slammed into the ground and walls, missing by inches. Mado moved like smoke—untouchable, smiling the whole time.

Tadanaka and Kume stood shocked. They could not believe what they were seeing. They had fought Kanaja with everything they had. And now...Mado was playing with her.

"He's not even trying," Kume whispered.

"He's untouchable..." Tadanaka added, voice low with disbelief.

Ina said nothing. She stood still, arms folded, eyes locked on Kanaja, her lips pressed into a tight line.

Then suddenly—her patience snapped.

"Forget that fool! Fight me," she shouted, her voice cutting through the chaos.

Kanaja turned.

A flash of lightning exploded from Ina's body. An explosion of electricity cracking through the air. Her hand hovered near her sword's hilt—and then she vanished.

She reappeared behind Kanaja in an instant, now kneeling, eyes closed. Lightning arced across her body, her blade only half-drawn.

Kanaja frozen in her place, still staring at where Ina had once stood. A moment of silence. Then, slowly—Ina exhaled.

Click.

Her sword settled fully into its sheath.

And in that moment, Kanaja's head exploded, a clean, sudden blast of lightning rupturing it from the inside out. Her body fell in one piece. She collapsed without sound.

Tadanaka and Kume stood in stunned silence. They didn't even see the strike.

"So this...this is the power of the Nokuba..." Kume whispered.

Mado scratched his head and started chuckling. "Scary, isn't she?" he said with a laugh.

Ina turned slowly, walking towards him. "What did I tell you about playing with your enemies?"

"Alright, alright, I know, no more games. Maybe," Mado said, raising both hands.

They walked away together, calm as ever.

Tadanaka and Kume didn't move. They couldn't. They were still trying to absorb what they had just witnessed. Power. Precision. Control. Unity. The Nokuba weren't just warriors. They were on another level.

"Now you know why joining the Nokuba is my dream?" Tadanaka whispered.

"Yes," Kume said quietly, eyes still fixed on Mado and Ina's backs.

Mado looked over his shoulder. "Our mission is done. We have to report to Lord Ryoze. Let's move."

CHAPTER TWENTY-FOUR
His Smile

A few days had passed. Laya sat alone in her temple, the silence stretching around her like a weight she couldn't shake. The halls were empty, the stone walls cold, but the noise was all in her head. Her thoughts wouldn't stop. She tried to meditate, to refocus, but it was useless. Ever since her visit to the Toukan castle, Yasaze had been stuck in her mind like a splinter she couldn't pull out.

It didn't make sense. She was a Member of the Obake—one of the strongest beings alive, feared by warriors across the land. She had killed without hesitation before, even watched her enemies beg for mercy. But when it came to Yasaze, she couldn't bring herself to even imagine harming him. No matter how many times she told herself he was just a human, just a weakness to be exploited, the thought of his smile—so unguarded, so genuine—kept returning. And every time it did, it chipped away at the walls she had spent years building.

Suddenly, the quiet was broken by a voice calling out from somewhere beyond the temple's entrance. It was faint at first, but persistent— someone was shouting her name. Laya stood immediately, her body tense as she moved toward the sound. Her senses were sharp, alert for danger. She stepped outside, eyes scanning the forest's edge.

There, standing just beyond the temple's steps, was Yasaze.

"Laya! There you are!" he called, waving both arms as if she hadn't already spotted him.

Laya's expression dropped into a glare. "What the hell are you doing here?" she asked, stepping toward him. "And how did you even find this place?"

Yasaze shrugged, unfazed by her tone. "I went to town a few times, hoping to see you again, but you never showed up. I started getting worried. So I tried to figure out where you might have gone. Every time we parted, I noticed you'd walk in this direction, deeper into the woods. I thought maybe you lived out here. So...I gave it a shot. And look—it worked."

"You got worried?" Laya repeated, crossing her arms. "You do realize I could kill an entire army of Reiki warriors by myself, right?"

Yasaze gave a short laugh, completely unaffected. "Yeah, yeah. I didn't mean I was worried you'd get hurt. I meant I was worried you'd feel lonely. And that's where I come in—to rescue you from boredom." He smiled at her again, that same light-hearted, sincere expression she couldn't seem to ignore.

Laya looked away, annoyed that her guard had slipped even for a second. *"There it is again,"* she thought. *"That stupid innocent smile."*

"If 'rescuing me' means coming here to annoy me, I'm fine, thanks," she muttered, turning around and heading back toward the temple.

"Wait, wait!" Yasaze called, jogging up behind her. "There's a festival tomorrow in the northeast region—fireworks, games, everything! Come with me!"

"Get lost, kid," Laya said flatly, not even turning around as she stepped through the entrance.

To her irritation, Yasaze followed her inside. He looked around curiously, completely ignoring the chill in her tone.

"So this is where you live?" he said, glancing around with a smirk. "Why is it so empty in here? Don't tell me you just sit around and stare at the walls all day."

Laya clenched her jaw, already regretting that she let him step inside.

"I mean, I can't even see a bed," Yasaze continued as he wandered deeper in. "Please don't tell me you don't have a bed. Wait...do Mutants even sleep? I've always wondered—"

"Enough," Laya snapped, her voice cutting clean through his chatter. "Fine. I'll go with you tomorrow. Just stop talking and get out, you little shit."

Yasaze blinked, then smiled like he'd just won a game. "Great. Meet me by the lake tomorrow morning," he said cheerfully.

And just like that, he turned and walked off, still smiling to himself, leaving Laya standing alone once more.

She stared after him in silence. She didn't know what bothered her more—the fact that he'd found her sanctuary so easily...or the fact that she'd agreed to go with him.

The next morning at the Toukan main castle, Yasaze woke before sunrise. The moment his eyes opened, he sat up with energy he rarely had. Today wasn't like every other day spent within the castle walls. Today was the festival—and more importantly, he was meeting Laya. The thought alone had him dressed and out the door in moments. He tied his sash quickly, pulled on his cloak, and rushed down the corridor with barely a glance behind him.

As he reached the outer gates, two familiar figures stepped into his path—his assigned bodyguards, Niko and Tin. Both were tall, disciplined men who had served the Toukan family for years. They knew Yasaze's routines better than anyone, rarely leaving his side.

"There you are," Niko said, folding his arms. "Where are you off to in such a hurry, Master Yasaze?"

"Oh, right," Yasaze said quickly, not missing a beat. "I was just with my father. He said he needed to speak with both of you. You should head over to him now—he's waiting in his chamber."

Niko and Tin exchanged a brief look, then nodded. "Understood," Niko replied, and both turned at once, walking back toward the inner halls.

As soon as they were out of sight, Yasaze smiled to himself, proud of his clever escape. "That should keep them busy for a while," he muttered under his breath, turning swiftly and slipping through the gates into the woods. The path toward the lake was quiet, just as he remembered. Trees stood tall around him, soft light filtering through the canopy above. He quickened his pace, excited and a little nervous.

But back inside the castle, Niko and Tin hadn't gone far. In fact, they hadn't gone anywhere at all. The moment they were out of Yasaze's sight, they stopped walking.

"He thinks he fooled us," Niko said, glancing over his shoulder with a small smirk. "He doesn't realize we were just with Master Yuuta five minutes ago."

Tin blinked, confused. "Wait...then why didn't we stop him?"

Niko looked at him patiently. "Because, Tin, it's obvious where he's going.

He's headed to meet that woman again."

"You mean that lady he's always talking to?" Tin asked. "Come on, it's not like they're in love or something. She's way older than him, and he's still young."

Niko sighed. "That's not what I meant, you idiot," he said calmly. "You and I have been guarding Yasaze since he was a boy. You know how he's always been—isolated, quiet, left out. No Reiki, no role in the family…He's kind, but he's lonely. That woman—Shiro or whatever her name is—she talks to him like he matters. She listens to him. She treats him like someone worth being around."

Tin scratched his head, his tone softening. "So…like a best friend?"

Niko nodded. "Exactly. He's just happy when he's with her. And honestly? I didn't want to ruin that for him. But we'll still follow him. Quietly. Just to make sure he's safe."

"Yeah, alright," Tin said with a grin. "Let's go."

With that, the two guards turned around and exited the castle once more, this time moving swiftly and quietly into the woods—keeping just far enough behind Yasaze not to be seen, but never far enough to lose sight of him.

Yasaze moved quickly through the woods, slipping between trees and over roots with quiet urgency. Sunlight pushed through the branches above, but he didn't slow down. He was late.

"She's going to kill me," he muttered.

He picked up the pace. The thought of Laya waiting by the lake, arms crossed and already annoyed, made him uneasy. She always seemed irritated around him, and now he was giving her a real reason.

"I'm almost there," he said to himself.

As Yasaze rounded a narrow bend in the path, something swept across his foot.

He didn't see it coming.

His body dropped hard to the ground, face hitting the dirt, arms scraping against loose stone. He let out a sharp breath, surprised and confused. Pushing himself up with a grunt, he turned his head to see what had tripped him.

A figure stood over him. A Mutant.

Pale skin. Hairless. Tall and still. His green eyes glowed faintly under the trees, sharp and unblinking. He didn't speak right away—he just smiled calmly, as if he'd been waiting for this moment.

Yasaze's body tensed. He quickly stood, brushing off his clothes, but his hands trembled slightly. His eyes avoided the Mutant's for a second too long.

"I'm sorry," he said, clearly nervous.

Jin's eyes narrowed slightly, picking up on the fear. The smile remained. "Don't worry," he said smoothly. "I'm not going to hurt you. You don't even have Reiki, so there's no reason. No fun in killing someone like you."

Yasaze didn't reply.

And the smile on the Mutant's face didn't fade.

Yasaze didn't speak. He stood there for another few seconds, trying to steady his breath. The Mutant hadn't moved, but his presence felt heavier than before, as if he were waiting for something.

"I should get going," Yasaze finally said. "I'm meeting someone, and I'm already late."

The Mutant's smile twitched slightly, but he stayed still, not moving an inch.

"A friend?" the Mutant asked.

Yasaze nodded. "Yeah."

"Interesting."

The Mutant looked him over one more time, his green eyes steady.

"You're really not hiding anything?" he asked. "No tricks. No power."

Yasaze forced a small smile, trying to stay polite. "I don't have anything to hide."

There was a pause. Then the Mutant raised his hand slightly and motioned forward, as if giving Yasaze permission to leave.

"Then go," he said. "You've got nothing I want."

Without another word, Yasaze turned and began walking.

As he stepped forward, he let out a quiet breath, trying to shake the tension from his shoulders. Leaves shifted softly beneath his feet. "Now I'm really late. How am I even going to explain this to Laya?" he said to himself.

Then it happened. He didn't get to take another step. Something tore into him from behind with brutal force. A deep, sharp pain exploded through his chest, cutting through him so suddenly it stole the air from his lungs.

His eyes went wide. He looked down. A clawed hand had pierced straight through him.

For a moment, he couldn't move. Couldn't speak. The warmth of his own blood spread across his chest, soaking through his clothes.

He opened his mouth, but no words came—only a strained breath and the taste of iron.

The claw pulled out, slow and steady. His knees gave out. He dropped to the ground, his hands hitting the dirt weakly before his body followed.

Everything was quiet again, except for the sound of his own shallow gasps.

Yasaze dragged himself through the dirt, his fingers slipping in the blood pooling beneath him. Every movement was agony. His arms trembled. His body shook. The pain in his chest made it hard to breathe, but some part of him refused to stop. He didn't know where he was crawling. He just knew he had to keep moving.

Footsteps approached from behind. Slow. Measured. Calm. Then a shadow passed over him. A hand wrapped around his neck, lifting him clean off the ground.

Yasaze gasped, legs dangling, blood pouring freely from his chest. His eyes widened in panic as he looked up at the Mutant holding him. The Mutant stared back with a faint, amused grin curling at the edges of his lips—not just entertained, but sinister, like a predator toying with prey. There was no rush in his movements, no urgency in his grip—only satisfaction in watching Yasaze suffer.

"Why...?" Yasaze choked out. "Please...let me go..."

The Mutant's expression didn't change.

"Laya should've killed you a while back," he said. "But she's getting soft."

Yasaze's eyes went wide. "Laya...?" he whispered. "You...you know her?"

The Mutant started laughing, as if amused by the surprise.

Yasaze's voice trembled, his heart pounding with confusion and fear. "Who...who are you?"

"I'm Jin," he replied coldly. "Third Member of the Obake."

Without waiting another moment, he turned and flung Yasaze through the air.

Yasaze hit the ground hard, rolling until his body slammed into the base of a tree. Pain exploded through him. He lay there for a moment, unmoving.

Then—slowly—his arms began to move again. He clawed at the dirt, dragging his broken body forward through the leaves and blood.

Tears mixed with the blood on his face as he cried out, his voice raw and breaking.

"Father...Ryoze...please...help me..."

But no one came. No one could hear him. Yasaze couldn't crawl anymore.

His arms gave out, his chest barely rising, the warmth of his blood seeping into the forest floor. Every part of him ached. Every breath was shallow, trembling.

The world was growing dimmer, the trees above fading into blurred outlines. But still, he stayed awake.

Jin stood over him in silence, towering and unmoved.

Yasaze turned his head slightly. His eyes were heavy, but they held no anger. No hatred. Only the same quiet light they always had.

And then...he smiled. That same gentle, innocent smile. The one that made every Reiki warrior around him want to protect him.

The one that made even Laya—a Member of the Obake—hesitate.

A smile of innocence that never belonged in a world like this.

Yasaze looked up at Jin. He was trembling. Bleeding. Powerless. And yet, he still smiled as he spoke.

"We're all meant to die someday…" he said, voice low and steady. He didn't say it to be brave. He didn't say it to be defiant. He said it because it was true. And because he had nothing left to fear.

Jin didn't reply. He raised his arm. And then he struck. The final blow landed without mercy.

Yasaze didn't scream. He didn't beg. He simply…stopped. His body went still in the dirt.

The blood beneath him no longer moved. And yet his face remained unchanged. That smile was still there—fragile, pure, unshaken.

Yasaze Toukan was dead.

The only soul in Alard born without Reiki…the only one who never belonged to a world of power, blades, or hatred…died alone in the woods.

Smiling.

CHAPTER TWENTY-FIVE
Rage and Grief

Deeper in the woods, not far from where Yasaze's lifeless body lay, two figures stood hidden among the trees. Niko and Tin, the two guards who had watched over him since he was a child, had seen everything unfold before their eyes. From the moment they followed him out of the castle, they kept their distance as they always did, allowing him the illusion of freedom he so often cherished. But this time was different. This time, freedom had cost too much.

They had arrived just in time to witness the attack—just in time to see a pale Mutant lift Yasaze by the throat like a ragdoll. They heard Yasaze's pleading voice, watched his blood spill onto the forest floor, and still...they didn't move.

It wasn't weakness. It wasn't hesitation. It was something worse—pure, consuming fear. Jin's Dark Reiki filled the forest like a storm, pressing against their skin and sinking into their bones. Neither of them had ever felt anything like it. It crushed every thought, silenced every instinct. Their bodies refused to listen, locked in place by a presence so oppressive it felt as though their souls had been paralyzed.

They wanted to scream, to run to Yasaze and shield him with their lives, but they remained frozen—horrified and trembling, forced to watch the boy they had sworn to protect die, helpless and alone.

Then it was over. The forest went quiet. Yasaze's body no longer moved, and the trail of blood that followed him came to its end. Still they stood there, unable to speak, unable to process what they had just witnessed. The only thing that remained in the air was grief—cold and unbearable.

Far from the scene, near the lake where they had agreed to meet, Laya sat alone on a flat stone, arms crossed and eyes fixed on the water. Her brows were drawn tight with irritation, but behind the frustration lingered something else—a strange unease she couldn't explain. She let out a sharp sigh, tapping her foot against the stone beneath her.

"I can't believe I agreed to go to some stupid festival," she muttered, scowling. "And now I'm sitting here like an idiot. Who does he think he is, making me wait?"

She stood, fully prepared to walk away. But after a few steps, she stopped and looked back at the lake. Her eyes lingered on the path where Yasaze was supposed to appear, and something in her chest twisted—not anger, not annoyance...something softer.

"I'll wait just a little bit more," she mumbled to herself, her voice quieter now.

She sat back down. Her thoughts drifted, unaware that the boy who always found his way to her, no matter how clumsy or late, would not be coming this time. The one person who made her forget what she was—the one who had made her hesitate—now lay still in the forest, far beyond her reach.

In the quiet of the Toukan main castle, Yuuta sat with Shita inside his private chamber, the two engaged in quiet but serious discussion.

But then, the silence broke. Muffled shouting echoed from beyond the chamber doors. Footsteps. Urgent. Fast. Growing louder.

Yuuta and Shita turned toward the door, eyes narrowing as the noise drew closer. There was no knock—only the sudden, jarring rasp as the doors slid open.

Niko stumbled in, his face streaked with panic and tears. Behind him, several Reiki warriors rushed in, immediately bowing low before Yuuta.

"Master Yuuta," one of them said breathlessly. "We're sorry—we tried to stop him, but he slipped past us."

Shita rose to her feet, furious. "How dare you enter without permission!" she snapped, her voice sharp and commanding.

Niko dropped to his knees at once, his head bowed so low it touched the ground. "Master...forgive me...please forgive me..." His voice cracked as he trembled, unable to lift his head.

Yuuta and Shita exchanged a glance. The fury in Shita's eyes faded, replaced by unease. Yuuta's brows furrowed. Something was wrong. Deeply wrong.

"What is it?" Shita demanded, stepping forward. "What's going on?!"

Niko sobbed once before forcing the name out.

"Yasaze..."

Yuuta froze. His entire body stiffened at the sound of his son's name.

But Niko couldn't continue. He broke into more apologies, barely able to speak. Yuuta didn't shout. He didn't even raise his voice. He simply stood and walked forward, stopping directly in front of Niko.

His voice was quiet, level, and low.

"What happened to Yasaze?" he asked. He didn't look at Niko. His gaze was fixed on the floor, as if bracing himself for the answer.

Niko's throat clenched, but he forced himself to say the words.

"He's been killed...by Jin. One of the Obake..."

The world went silent.

Yuuta didn't react at first. He didn't speak. He didn't even breathe.

Then, slowly, his knees gave out beneath him, and he dropped fully to the floor, hands resting limp at his sides.

Shita stared, stunned. "No..." she whispered.

But denial gave way to fury. She marched toward Niko and grabbed him by the front of his robe, dragging him up slightly. Her voice broke as she screamed.

"What are you saying?! What do you mean he's been killed?! What kind of joke is this?!" Tears were already falling freely down her face. "You idiot, tell me it's not true!"

Niko didn't answer. He didn't fight. He just wept.

Yuuta remained silent.

Then, slowly, he raised a hand—a quiet signal.

Shita's voice faltered. She released her grip on Niko and stepped back, wiping at her tears, biting down hard to keep herself from sobbing.

Yuuta finally spoke, his voice hollow.

"Where is he?"

Niko swallowed hard. "I...I took him to the Infirmary."

Yuuta nodded once, though his eyes still hadn't lifted from the floor.

And the chamber fell into heavy silence once more.

Yuuta and Shita left without another word, their steps quick but heavy as they moved through the castle halls. No one stopped them. No one dared. The tension around them was thick and suffocating. When they reached the Infirmary, a silence hung in the air like a curtain. Every doctor present stood motionless. No one met their eyes. Heads were lowered. Faces pale.

Yuuta stepped forward slowly. His voice, when he spoke, was barely more than a whisper.

"Where is my son...?"

The head doctor didn't speak. He simply turned his head toward the far room—a small, private space at the end of the corridor.

Yuuta walked ahead without waiting. Shita followed, her feet dragging as she neared the doorway. The quiet inside was deeper than before, as if the room itself were holding its breath.

There was a single bed at the center. A body lay on it, covered head to toe in a white sheet.

Shita stopped at the threshold, frozen.

Yuuta took another step. Then another. He stood at the edge of the bed, the still form before him. His hand hovered in the air, trembling slightly. For a moment, he did nothing. Then he released a long, slow breath, reached down, and carefully pulled the sheet back.

There he was. Yasaze. Still. Lifeless. Peaceful.

Yuuta didn't speak. He didn't cry. He didn't fall to the floor. He just stood there, staring down at his son—the youngest of his blood, the one who had no power but all the kindness this world never deserved.

Behind him, Shita saw Yasaze's face beneath the sheet, and everything inside her shattered. She collapsed to her knees before she could stop herself, hands covering her mouth as the first sob tore through her chest. Then another. And another. The tears came faster than she could wipe them away. Her voice cracked as she broke down beside the doorway, her cries echoing softly against the stone walls.

Yuuta didn't move. He just stood in silence, his eyes fixed on Yasaze's face, as if waiting for his son to open his eyes again.

But he never did. Yuuta didn't move from his place beside the bed. His hand rested gently on the sheet that now covered Yasaze again, his gaze fixed on the face he would never see open its eyes. His voice, when it finally came, was soft—calm, but hollow.

"Send word to Ryoze. And Tadanaka. And to every corner of Alard. Let the entire land know…"

He paused only briefly, as if saying it made it real.

"…Yasaze is dead."

He never looked up. He never looked away.

Messengers were dispatched at once. Word traveled like wind over the mountains, crossing villages and clans, carried by messengers and wings. The news spread quickly, silence following wherever it landed.

At Ryoze's castle, a lone messenger made his way to the gates. His face was pale, his expression tight. Naru happened to be walking near the entrance when she noticed him. One look at his face, and she knew.

Something was wrong. Deeply wrong.

She approached him immediately, her tone sharp. "You're looking for Ryoze?"

The messenger nodded but didn't speak. Naru's eyes narrowed. She didn't wait for more.

Ryoze appeared not long after, having noticed their exchange. He walked toward them, his expression unreadable.

"What's this about?" he asked.

The messenger hesitated, swallowing hard. His voice faltered for a moment as he opened his mouth. Then he spoke the words he had carried for miles.

"Lord Yasaze...has been killed."

Silence swallowed the moment.

Naru turned sharply to Ryoze, watching him carefully. His face had not moved. His expression didn't change. He stood there, staring at the messenger as if waiting for the real message to come.

But it didn't. There was no sound. No words. Just silence between all three of them. Then, without a word, Ryoze started to walk.

His steps were slow, steady, and deliberate. He walked past Naru, past the messenger, and down the long path that led to the main castle.

Naru didn't call after him. She just watched him go, because it was clear to her. Something inside him had just broken.

Moving quietly, she began walking beside him. He didn't look at her. He didn't speak. His eyes remained fixed straight ahead, unfocused, like he wasn't thinking—only walking.

And then, as the wind passed gently across the path, a single tear fell, and with it, part of him. He didn't wipe it away. He just kept walking.

At the Gochuu base, the sound of clashing practice weapons rang out through the training grounds. Tadanaka and the other Gochuu Members were midsession, sweat on their brows, focus in their eyes, each of them pushing themselves harder than usual. The atmosphere was sharp but light—they were warriors, but there was still room for laughter and strength in unity.

Then a figure appeared at the entrance. A lone messenger stood just outside the training field, his presence alone enough to attract everyone's attention. The weapons were lowered. The chatter stopped.

Tadanaka stepped forward, wiping his hands on a cloth, a light grin still on his face.

"What's going on?" he asked casually, walking toward the messenger. "You look like you've seen a ghost."

But the messenger didn't return the smile. He simply lowered his head, hesitated for a moment, then delivered the news.

The moment the words were spoken, Tadanaka froze. His expression drained of all color. Behind him, the others stood in stunned silence, unsure they had even heard correctly.

"What...what are you saying?" Tadanaka asked, his voice hollow, the weight of the words not yet settling in.

The messenger bowed his head further. "Yasaze...is dead."

Tadanaka's breath caught. His chest began to rise and fall faster, the air catching painfully in his lungs. His hands shook. He blinked rapidly, as if trying to make sense of the words.

Kume stepped forward with a stricken expression, gently placing a hand on his shoulder. She didn't say anything. She didn't have to. Her touch was steady—a silent attempt to ground him, to console, even though she herself was trembling.

The silence didn't last. Tadanaka suddenly started running, his movements urgent and uneven. The rest of the Gochuu followed immediately.

None of them spoke.

They all rushed together toward the main castle, a sense of dread gripping their hearts as they moved, hoping—desperately—that somehow, it wasn't true.

The news spread quickly, faster than any wind across Alard. Village to village, district to district—whispers turned into cries, cries into silence. By midday, crowds had begun forming in front of the Toukan main castle. Men, women, children, and warriors alike gathered with heavy hearts, some in disbelief, others openly mourning. The youngest son of Lord Yuuta—the only Toukan born without Reiki, beloved by many—was gone.

Far from the castle, still waiting by the lake, Laya sat with her arms crossed and her patience long worn thin. Her eyes narrowed at the path that remained empty.

"That idiot," she muttered, rising to her feet. "He made me wait long enough. When I find him, I'll break his legs and make him regret the day he ever invited me."

She dusted herself off and turned to leave, heading back down the familiar path through the woods. As she neared the town, the sound of hurried footsteps and raised voices caught her attention. Stepping closer, she found herself facing a rush of townspeople—everyone seemed to be running in the same direction. The streets, normally quiet at this hour, were filled with urgency and tension. Confused, Laya grabbed a woman by the arm as she passed.

"What's going on?" she asked.

The woman, breathless and pale, barely slowed her pace. "Haven't you heard?

Lord Yasaze...he's dead. The youngest son of Yuuta—they say he was killed. Everyone's gathering at the main castle."

And with that, the woman pulled away and continued on.

Laya didn't move. She couldn't. The words echoed in her head like a bell that wouldn't stop ringing.

Yasaze. Dead.

Her legs gave out beneath her, and she dropped to her knees in the middle of the street, unaware of the people rushing past her on all sides. Her expression was blank at first—lips parted, eyes wide—as if her mind couldn't quite accept what she'd just heard. She sat there in the dirt, unmoving, caught between disbelief and something deeper.

Then the grief started to settle. A tightness in her chest. A sting behind her eyes.

He was gone. The boy who never judged her. Who smiled without reason. Who talked to her like she wasn't a Mutant.

The only one who ever made her forget what she was. Gone. Her fingers curled in the dirt. Her hands trembled. The pain didn't disappear—but it began to change. It twisted into something hotter. Heavier. It burned in her chest like fire clawing to be let out. Her shoulders stiffened. Her breathing quickened. Her jaw clenched so tightly it hurt.

Then her expression shifted. The blankness drained away. What remained was fury.

Her eyes darkened, her lips pressed into a thin line, and her whole body tightened with barely contained anger. As she lifted her head slowly, the look in her eyes was no longer lost—it was sharp. Focused. Dangerous.

"Jin..." She rose from the ground, fists clenched at her sides, her entire frame shaking—no longer from sadness, but from rage.

"I swear...you'll pay for this." Her voice was low, but every word vibrated with venom. There was no hesitation now. Only wrath.

As Ryoze and Naru approached the Toukan main castle, the massive crowd gathered at the gates fell into silence. The muttering, the sobs, the whispered prayers—all stopped the moment they saw him. Ryoze walked through them without a word, his eyes fixed forward, his face unreadable. He didn't seem to notice the people at all. Their presence meant nothing to him now. All he could see was the path ahead.

Naru followed closely behind him, her steps steady, her gaze sharp. She, too, said nothing.

Shita turned the moment she heard the door slide open. Her eyes widened as she saw Ryoze step inside, and she rushed toward him. Her hands pressed gently against his chest, trying to stop him from moving forward.

"Ryoze..." she whispered, her voice thick with grief. "Don't go in there."

But he didn't look at her. His eyes never shifted. He stood still for a moment, then slowly reached up and moved her hands away, his touch careful.

"It's okay," he said softly. Then he walked past her.

Yuuta was already there, seated beside the body that lay beneath a clean white sheet. He didn't speak. His face held no expression, his posture heavy. He didn't look up when Ryoze approached.

Ryoze came to a stop beside his younger brother's body. He stared for a long time, unmoving. Then he knelt down and gently pulled the sheet back from Yasaze's face. His hand reached out, trembling slightly, and rested on Yasaze's cheek.

For the first time since hearing the news, Ryoze smiled—just barely. The tears broke through, tracing a slow path down his face. Then, quietly, his expression changed. The smile faded. His jaw tightened. His eyes darkened. And what remained was something far colder.

"Father," Ryoze said, voice low and sharp. "Who is responsible for this?"

Yuuta didn't lift his gaze. His voice was calm. "Jin. One of the Obake."

Ryoze didn't react. He remained still, hand still resting on Yasaze's face.

Yuuta finally looked up. "Niko was the one who brought the news. Tin—his other guard—followed Jin after the attack. He's trying to locate the Mutant's sanctuary."

The silence that followed was thick with tension. Ryoze said nothing.

The silence inside the Infirmary was suddenly shattered by the sound of hurried footsteps pounding down the corridor. The door slammed open and Tadanaka burst breathlessly into the room, his voice cracking as he shouted.

"Yasaze!"

His eyes scanned the room until they landed on the body lying still beneath the white sheet. His heart dropped. No one answered him. No one tried to stop him. He rushed forward, collapsing beside his younger brother's body.

"No, no, come on—wake up," he pleaded, his hands shaking as he touched Yasaze's arm, then his face. "Please, Yasaze. Don't do this... don't leave us like this..."

The sound of his sobs filled the room. Loud. Raw. Every emotion poured out of him—heartbreak, disbelief, helplessness. His body trembled as he leaned over Yasaze's lifeless form, tears falling freely down his cheeks as he cried his brother's name again and again.

Yuuta didn't move. Ryoze didn't speak.

They just stood in silence, watching as the weight of the loss broke Tadanaka, who now wept over his brother's lifeless body.

After a long moment, Ryoze finally stepped forward. Walking slowly and quietly, he knelt behind Tadanaka. His hand rested gently on his brother's shoulder—firm, steady, but wordless. It was all he could offer.

Then, without a sound, Ryoze rose to his feet and walked out of the room, his footsteps echoing softly down the hall.

He didn't look back. Because if he did, he might not be able to keep walking.

Night had settled over the Toukan main castle, casting long shadows across its halls. Inside one of the quiet rooms, the Members of the Nokuba sat together—all of them present, except for Ryoze.

No one spoke. The room was heavy with silence, the kind that made every breath feel like an interruption. Each of them wore the same expression—grief, restraint, and uncertainty. None of them knew what to say, and for a while, it felt like there was nothing to say at all.

Then Mado stood abruptly, the silence broken by the sharp edge of his voice.

"Enough. I've had it," he snapped. "I'm going out there to find that Jin bastard and bring his head back myself."

Before he could take another step, Naru's voice cut in, calm but firm. "Sit down, Mado. We don't have orders to move."

He turned toward her, his fists clenched, shoulders still tense. But when he spoke again, his anger wavered—replaced by something deeper.

"Lord Ryoze is suffering," he said quietly. "He lost his little brother, and he's keeping it all inside. And we're just sitting here, doing nothing. You really expect me to be okay with that?"

No one replied. They didn't need to.

Because every single one of them felt it—the same ache, the same guilt, the same helplessness. Their thoughts weren't just on revenge or duty. They were on Ryoze. Their leader.

They were all worried. And none of them knew how to ease the pain he carried.

Just then, the door opened.

They turned as one. The moment they saw who had entered, every one of them rose to their feet and dropped to one knee, forming a line across the room in silent respect.

Master Yuuta stood in the doorway, quiet and composed, his presence effortlessly commanding. He looked at them for a long moment—no words, just a measured gaze—then finally spoke.

"Stand," he said. "All of you. Come with me."

Without question, they rose and followed.

CHAPTER TWENTY-SIX
Before the Storm

The woods were quiet, but Laya's footsteps were sharp, deliberate. She moved through the trees without a word, but inside, the rage burned hotter with every step. Her jaw was tight, her eyes fixed ahead, and the weight in her chest had turned into something volatile.

She didn't slow down as she neared her temple. She already knew he would be there. The moment she stepped inside, her eyes confirmed what her instincts had already told her—Jin was waiting.

He sat at the center of the temple, legs crossed, posture relaxed, hands resting casually in his lap. That same amused, detached smile was stretched across his face. As if he'd been expecting her all along.

Back at the main castle, Yuuta moved steadily through the corridors, his footsteps slow but certain. The Members of the Nokuba followed him in silence, their presence unified and solemn behind him. No one spoke. The halls, usually filled with voices and motion, now felt hollow.

As they turned a corner, they came upon Tadanaka and the Gochuu Members.

Tadanaka stood with his head lowered, shoulders trembling, eyes still wet with grief. The Gochuu surrounded him, quiet and close, offering what little comfort they could. None of them had words that would ease what he felt—but their presence said enough.

When they saw Yuuta and the Nokuba approaching, the Gochuu dropped to one knee in unison. Tadanaka followed a second later, still wiping his face with his sleeve.

Yuuta stepped forward, his expression softening as he reached out and placed a hand on his son's shoulder.

"Rise, Tadanaka," he said gently.

Tadanaka lifted his head slowly, meeting his father's eyes.

"Go back to your base, son," Yuuta said, a faint, reassuring smile tugging at his lips. "Everything will be alright."

Tadanaka hesitated for a moment, then nodded. He didn't speak, just turned quietly. The Gochuu followed him down the corridor, their steps heavy with grief.

As soon as they disappeared from view, the brief smile faded from Yuuta's face. The warmth drained from his expression, replaced by something cold, focused.

Without another word, he turned and resumed walking toward his chamber, the Nokuba Members still following him.

When they entered Yuuta's chambers, the light inside was dim and still. Hala, his granddaughter, was already asleep, curled beneath the covers, her small frame rising and falling with each quiet breath. Yuuta walked over slowly and sat beside her, watching her in silence. For a moment, the hard lines of his face softened. The weight of his title, his grief, and the burden of what lay ahead all seemed to lift, if only slightly, as he looked at his granddaughter resting peacefully in his bed.

Then he rose, turning to face the Nokuba, who had all dropped to one knee behind him in silent respect.

"You are to stay here tonight," Yuuta said. "Protect the castle—and the glass plate—until I return."

The Nokuba didn't hesitate. "Understood, Master!" they said in unison, their voices clear and resolute.

Yuuta stepped past the Nokuba without a word and quietly left his chambers. The halls of the castle stretched before him, empty and dim, each footstep echoing faintly behind him. He walked slowly, alone, his back straight, but his shoulders heavy with grief.

With every step, memories began to rise.

Yasaze's voice. His laughter. That innocent, clumsy smile that had no place in a world like this. Flashes of him—running through the courtyard, laughing too loudly at things others would ignore, sitting beside him in silence as if he belonged there without needing permission.

Yuuta's pace slowed. The air froze in his lungs. Then his legs gave way just slightly.

He stumbled, reaching out to brace himself against the wall. His palm pressed hard into the cold surface, his head bowed. And then, without sound, the tears came. They slipped down his face, unhidden, unstoppable. He clenched his jaw and forced the breath back into his lungs. He gathered himself, straightened, and kept walking.

He passed through the inner gates of the castle and made his way down the long path leading out into the woods. The cold air hit him, but it wasn't enough to ground him. He couldn't shake the pain that throbbed in his chest.

And that was when another memory surfaced—one older than the rest...

His wife, Lady Tala, lying on her deathbed. Her voice weak, but her words clear.

"Yuuta...he may not have Reiki, but he's still our son. Don't let anyone treat him as less—promise me you'll protect him."

And then she turned her head and looked at Ryoze and Shita—so young back then—her voice barely a whisper.

"And you two...watch over your brother. He'll need you more than you know."

The memory faded like smoke, and Yuuta's steps slowed. He stopped in the middle of the wooded path, surrounded by darkness.

"I'm sorry, Tala..." he murmured, his voice broken. "I couldn't protect our son." For a moment, he stood there in despair. Then something in his eyes changed. The grief didn't vanish, but it hardened. It became rage. He looked up, and his voice came low, steady, and colder than ever before.

"But I will avenge him." He took another step forward, and his voice rang out into the darkness. "Let's go."

From the shadows, two figures emerged—one to his right, another to his left.

Ryoze. Shita. Neither said a word. It was as if they had been waiting for him all along. The three of them walked side by side into the night—no banners, no warriors, no noise. Just the sound of their footsteps and the weight of vengeance burning in their silence.

As their figures disappeared into the darkened woods, one truth burned in the air: The time for mourning was over.

The war had just begun...

AUTHOR BIO

M.J.Saeed

M.J. Saeed is a fantasy author from the UAE and the creator of *Toukan*, his debut novel. Set in a world of powerful clans, dark secrets, and Reiki-fueled conflict, his stories blend emotion, intensity, and purpose. What began as a quiet vision grew into a saga that refused to stay unwritten.